Originally from Lor
moved to rural North Sweden in the spring of 2020
to pursue her dream of writing full-time.

An alumna of For Books' Sake's Write Like A Grrrl
and Comma Press Short Story courses, she was
longlisted for the Commonwealth Short Story Prize
2021 and shortlisted for the Cambridge Short Story
Prize 2021. *Tools For Surviving a Storm* is Nadia's
debut collection of short stories.

NADIA HENDERSON

# TOOLS FOR SURVIVING A STORM

First published in Great Britain in 2021 by Dear Damsels

Copyright © Nadia Henderson, 2021

ISBN 978-1-8381-6611-3

Printed and bound in Great Britain by Clays Ltd, Elcograf S.p.A.


Dear Damsels
www.deardamsels.com

'I'm not afraid of storms,
for I'm learning how to sail my ship.'

Louisa May Alcott, *Little Women*

# Her Child is Born
# On a Sunday

Her child is born on a Sunday, one week late. He is born with every finger and toe, wet with a coat of soft down. She doesn't sleep the night he arrives, but he does: he slips, mouth at her breast, into slumber, and she counts his fingers, his toes, brings her lips to the crown of his head, to that sweet, soft down.

She dreams a lot in the beginning. Drops of blood in snow, the crushed bodies of dead birds around the house. In one dream, she hears her son crying but can't get to him. She runs down an endless corridor, opening each door to an empty crib. It is hardest six weeks in, when Zach leaves for work. It's already been three days but still, when she wakes, she turns to his side of the bed expecting warmth to find only the cold, creased sheet.

She rests the phone between her face and the pillow, cups her hand over the speaker.

His voice is a thorn. 'It's 4 a.m. here.'

She imagines the hotel room dark and soulless around him, his suitcase open at the end of the bed, dress shoes lined up by the door. 'I'm sorry. I had another dream.'

There's a rustling sound. 'Which one?'

'The bad one.'

They lie in their respective beds, thousands of miles apart, and see the same thing: their baby, asleep in his crib, the black cloud of hornets moving closer, faster than they can, their imaginary legs like splinters in honey.

She winds fabric around her son, binds him to her front and knots the wrap below him. His hand paws at her jumper, to the sustenance beneath it for which he seems to have an endless thirst. The wind in the pine trees sounds like a stream as they move into the woods behind the house, snow crunching underfoot. They don't go far, venturing only to a clearing a few minutes' walk away; she looks back to be sure that, from here, she can still see the plume of smoke rising from the chimney.

She sees the hare when she turns back around, a few metres away by the edge of the clearing. Its fur, pale for the winter, is coarse against the expanse of snow. It stands side on, ears pricked; even from this distance, she can see its heart beating below the rough coat, nose twitching. It knows it's being watched, but more – it stands with the vigilant unease of a creature hunted.

Her son twists in his wrap, feet kicking against her. He is desperate to reach his arms towards the animal. He gurgles, innocent curiosity mixed with something else – something instinctual. She brings a finger to his mouth to soothe him and he bites. A shock of pain runs through her; she snatches her hand away and sees pearls of blood budding on the surface of her skin. She looks up and the hare is gone.

When they return to the house, she lays her son down in his crib and prises his small mouth open. She feels the teeth before she sees them: a neat row on each gum, punctuated by four jagged fangs.

Zach doesn't pick up on the first ring. She doesn't stop to check what time it is there. She calls back straight away and he answers. 'Is everything OK?'

'He bit me,' she says.

His voice is brittle with weariness. 'Listen, I've just got to the airport and they're saying the flight is delayed. There's a snowstorm blowing in from the coast – it could be a while.'

She presses her thumb to the bandaged pad of her index finger, blotted seeds of blood. The line goes dead.

Later, she sits on the edge of the bed, spills herself into sterilised bottles.

She doesn't dream of the hornets or the blood but of a skinned hare standing in the bedroom doorway. Its stripped body glistens in sunlight, sinews stretched over muscles, protruding bones. Tufts of the sheared coat have settled at its feet. Its head, still – mercifully – furred, sits at an unnatural angle, the neck worked red. She wakes with the taste of bile in her throat.

From the crib, a low snarling. She walks to the kitchen, eyes down, and prepares a bottle of pumped milk. She is purposefully slow in her movements, basking in blissful pretence. There's a world, she thinks, in which her son has not grown a beast's teeth overnight at six weeks; some version of reality in which the flesh there is tender, unbroken. To whom, she wonders, must she offer her prayers in order to access that sacred place?

Reaching up from the crib is not the hand of a child. The perfect fingers, gone; replaced by a blackened stump from which yellowing claws curl out. She moves closer. Fur spreads down each limb; slick with newness, resplendent. She hadn't wanted the baby at first – a private, shameful truth – but now there's no sacrifice she wouldn't make to have her child returned to his rightful form. She grips the side of the crib and peers in. His cherubim face is peaked in a snout, button nose wet and rubbery. The fur is darker in the centre, smudging to a ring of light brown. The milk bottle rolls under the bed.

Her lungs bloat, breathing turns ragged. Zach does not pick up. She hurls the phone at the wall, watches the parts of it fall to the floor.

They'd not yet settled on a name. Conversations on the subject had quickly soured, each parent's suggestions met with indifference by the other. Reminder letters from the local authority had piled up, unopened. Now, she entertains the idea that his namelessness – their indecision – has left her son vulnerable to otherworldly intervention. There must, after all, be some explanation.

The day melts into evening. She's not sure how long she's been sitting outside the closed bedroom door. Her son is no longer crib-bound, confined by the normal measures of growth. She hears skittish claws across floorboards, a curious nose at the door frame. Guttural emissions signal his bodily needs; in response, circles of milk spoil at her breasts. Her mind fogs. Every solution to his hunger is unthinkable. With Zach away, she has indulged her preference for meat-free eating; nothing in the fridge will sate him. Then, she remembers: Zach's foray into game hunting last year, the rifles in the basement. Her stomach bristles.

Sleep drifts above her like a summer breeze, fleeting and fickle. She keeps a hand poised on the weapon, checking routinely that its mouth is pointing away from her. Her body aches from maintaining a cross-legged vigil on the floor by the bedroom door. Behind it, activity has slowed, but there's still a restless pacing, paws padding from one side of the room to the other. She can't bring herself to speak aloud – what if her voice were to elicit a response? – so she mouths a promise of provisions, vows to honour her motherly duties.

She sets off just before dawn. Leaving him alone in the house had been an exercise in reckoning with this harrowing truth that had almost been too much to bear. Even now as she strides towards the woods, there's the thought – and the rifle, compliant, at her side – but no. She sinks into a different fantasy: claws, fur, black nose, all reduced to the fodder of nightmares, her son's human assets restored as swiftly as they'd been forfeited.

The clearing expands, coated in milky darkness. Her tread is heavy, unbalanced; the quilted landscape conspiring, rejecting her presence. She searches for sound in impenetrable silence. From beyond the clearing, there's a rustling, and she imagines lean bodies twitching, necks craning to triangulate danger. The tip of the rifle glints.

She'd been raised in a place not dissimilar to this one, had hunted alongside her father. It was a gruesome business, she'd decided, but the method of it had lingered. And so, she knows how to scare up the fruits of the forest; she paces, then waits, trains her gun on the hallowed warren. Between moments, there's a split in the stillness – a time to squeeze gently, so gently, then release. Small creatures scatter into the undergrowth but she sees straight away that she's hit one: beads of red against white.

She's delirious with exhaustion, she knows, but is there not something poetic, fateful, in the fact she's hit the jill? One mother laying down her life for another. The hare's body lies among the collected debris of the form: a cradle of peeling twigs and frozen leaves, thinly covered in snow. Crouching beside it, she sees that her shot isn't clean. There's a sliver of life to which the animal clings, a weak but wilful breathing. The hare's neck is malleable under her fingers; she twists, and the bones snap like kindling. She lays the rifle down, scans the brambles for an offering to leave in exchange. Eventually, she lifts the carcass away, arranging in its place small stones in the shape of a cross.

Morning rolls in, slow and silken, as the house comes into view. She hadn't liked the idea of living so remotely at first, but she's thankful for it now. There's been a reconfiguration. Her blood, rerouted in her veins, seems to flow electric. Her senses are keenly alert, attuned to birdsong, the dawn light changing, death limp in the grip of her hand.

He's clawing at the bedroom door. She turns the handle with caution, but it's barely open an inch before a flurry of snout and teeth rip the hare away. She pushes the door open wider with the tip of her boot, registers torn sheets, felled curtains, feathers liberated from pillows. There's a rancid smell – animal but chemical. She watches her son, who'd suckled so sweetly mere days ago, tear flesh from bones in the corner of the room, behind his upended crib. This time, when she sinks to the floor, she does not close the door.

He lays waste to the house, paying her slumped body little attention. Books thud from shelves, framed photos shatter, potted plants toppled by the brush of a tail. It's an inquisitive destruction with no ill intention. She wonders how much of her child's mind remains; her six-week-old son, suddenly mobile with a world to explore. The exhilaration of the morning is waning; grief pulling like a tide, so tempting to succumb to. In lulls between consciousness, she sees hornets flicker in the hallway, defying the season. It's a lucid vision, she's certain: her son's wolven form at the front door. What she must do next feels inevitable.

There are parts she remembers. They float into her memory, fragmentary. Breadcrumb trail of tracks in the snow, the clearing like a day not yet sullied. Crusted blood at her cuticles, the arrangement of stones untouched. She recalls a familiar voice, fiercer than she's ever known it, several hands on her at once. The intervention felt euphoric, a blessed confirmation: this is over.

Strip lights blaze above her. She adjusts naked limbs against threadbare sheets, finds them bound. Beside her, a monitor displays lines and numbers, beeping routinely. Tubes run like veins down her arm. Suspended from the ceiling, a screen shows aerial scenes of a forest, the tops of pine trees tipped white. She sees her own home from a height, the footage circling, winding. Sirens glow fluorescent.

Her child was born on a Sunday, one week late. She waited for him in a bed like this one, whispered spells to coax him. His arrival was quick and fluid. What a treat he was, what a gift, with every finger and toe. A mother's dream.

# Mushroom Picking
# For Strangers

Tatiana Rusak was not supposed to be awake. It was quarter past midnight, and from the top of the stairs, she watched her father open the door to their neighbour, Stanislaŭ Vasilena. Stanislaŭ was not the kind of man you might expect to be able to run half a mile in below-zero temperatures, but there he stood, gasping for breath on the doorstep of the Rusaks' family farm. His was the only home in the village with a television. It was, he said, his duty to let the other farmers know what had happened at the nuclear plant across the border. He'd set off straight after the broadcast, despite his wife's protestations.

To scare Tatiana off staying up late, her mother had resorted to telling heavily embellished stories from the old religion: benevolent household spirits, angered by her bedtime rebellion, would forsake the farm, inviting in all manner of chaos. So, when Stanislaŭ's knock came downstairs, Tatiana wondered if the spirits had finally had enough of her nocturnal inclinations. Perhaps, she sometimes thinks, every terrible thing that happened next can be traced back to the sleepless nights of a nine-year-old girl.

Gert bends to tug the mushroom out of the ground at the base of its stem. He holds it up for Tatiana to see: a thick stem topped by a flat, brown cap. His fingernails are crusted with dirt, hands textured with age like the bark of the pine trees around them. '*Cortinarius rubellus*,' he says.

It's the first thing he's said to her since they set off an hour ago. They share English as a common second language but have, she thinks, different levels of willingness to use it. In the months since she arrived in Sweden, Tatiana has lived mostly in silence, speaking only when it's absolutely necessary at the migration office, or the supermarket, or as she sprays disinfectant onto the children's desks at the town's only school alongside the rest of the cleaners. Gert is just another quiet stranger whose silence is shyness at best, intolerance at worst.

'A *kantarell?*' she says.

Her case worker at the migration office had been the one to suggest she get involved with the local community. Surprised, Tatiana had asked if her application for permanent residence in the country depended on it. The case worker had laughed, a social cue that should have been the same in every language but that had left Tatiana unsure of the answer. To be safe, she'd trawled the online groups for the neighbourhood, landing on a mushroom-picking excursion that reminded her of a childhood spent in awe of the mystical shapes and patterns of the fungi that sprung from the ground in the woods around her family's farm. She hadn't anticipated being the only participant.

'No,' Gert says. It's hard to ignore the impatience in his voice. He pokes at the spongy cap. 'Too dark, wrong shape. Not a *kantarell*.'

Gert tosses the impersonator into a blueberry thicket. Tatiana wants to ask him if the mushrooms here are still radioactive. She read that, in the months after Chernobyl, Swedes were discouraged from picking berries and fungi in affected areas of the country. She wonders if Gert is aware of the important role his homeland played in forcing the Soviets to come clean about the disaster. She pads past where Gert is hunched, playing through their imagined conversation in her head. That's when she sees them, half buried in the plush bed of moss and leaves under her feet: golden chanterelles, their inverted caps reaching majestically skywards.

'*Kantarell*!' she says, stunned by the truth of her own excitement, eager to earn back Gert's respect. But no sooner has he risen up than he's drained of all colour and falls, heavy and fast, down to the forest floor.

It was the year ABBA had their first Eurovision victory. It was the year Lena Andersson transferred from Uppsala University, and so the year every guy – and some girls, too – lined up for the chance to latch onto her centre of gravity. Gert knew he was supposed to find Lena irresistible. He partook, shamefully, in the ritualistic scrutinising of her physical features, her various attributes appraised by the small circle of young men who'd become his closest friends. Among them, Emil Sandström, whose sharp jawline and pool-blue eyes inspired in Gert a desire so blinding he couldn't look at it directly, and wouldn't for another twenty years.

It had been at Emil's request that Gert had taken a bite of the mushroom. They'd flocked to a party Lena and her friends were throwing at her parents' summer cabin. On the decaying veranda,

Emil produced a paper bag with a single mushroom inside. Gert held the bulbous stem, probing its springy brown cap. *Cortinarius rubellus*. He knew it was toxic. But what harm would the smallest of nibbles, chased by a cleansing mouthful of vodka, really do? Maybe, in a fungi-induced fugue state, Emil would not object to Gert running a finger along the clean line of his jaw and straight into his open mouth. But no such reverie was realised. At that moment, Gert felt entirely unchanged.

It took several days for the sickness to set in. Gert attended his lectures, cycling through a campus whose trees were bejewelled with the warm tones of autumn. The thirst was the first sign to show, a want so strong it woke him in the night one week later. He filled up his glass in the kitchen and wondered if this was how it felt to die of unexpressed desire. No amount of water could quench him. Next day came the aches, his muscles tightening like ropes. Emil was absent from class. The ropes pulled tighter. By the third day, he'd barely left the bathroom before needing to go back in. To die like this felt mythical. A fabled death. He would follow the sound of strings to the lake, where Emil would be waiting, bow balanced on the bridge of his instrument, to sink quick as stones to the bottom.

In the ten or so seconds it takes for Gert to come round, Tatiana thinks of her father. He'd be around Gert's age if he was still alive, she thinks, analysing the depth of the lines around Gert's eyes and mouth, the soft hang of skin at his neck. Her father hadn't liked the city. In the flat they were moved to he'd paced like a bear in a cage, bated to violence by the slightest perceived misstep from Tatiana or her mother. Sometimes, she imagines the spirits of her mother's retelling leading him out onto the balcony. She wonders how he would have done it if they'd been put on the first floor instead of the sixth.

Gert is breathing very quickly. He opens and closes his eyes several times, a strand of saliva stretching between his parted lips. Tatiana pretends not to notice the dark spread of urine on his jeans. Above them, a breeze rustles the pines. 'You fainted,' she says, defaulting, as she always does when unsure what to say, to the facts.

'Yes, I know,' Gert says, propping himself up on his forearms. He sees he has wet himself, and that Tatiana has noticed. He'd always thought people from her part of the world were unnecesarily forthcoming with the truth, but in seeing how determined she is to keep her gaze averted he understands this judgement to be wrong. 'It happens sometimes.'

Tatiana stares at the forest floor, punctured with glinting gold. The stillness is absolute, ancient trees rooted in ancient land. She has practised stillness from the moment she got off the plane from Minsk. No sudden movements or unguarded glances that might tell of malevolent motives. At midnight in the school cafeteria, the small group of women snap open Tupperwares packed with baked goods that remind them of home. Within each of them a lifetime of stories exists. It is enough, though, the quiet exchange of edible memories, bleach-worn hands brushing in passing.

Gert glances round at the blanket of mushrooms beneath them. '*Herregud, vad mycket kantareller.*'

'Do you feel OK?' Tatiana asks. 'Should we leave?'

'I'm fine,' Gert says, his voice cushioned by the bed of moss.

Tatiana crouches in the middle of the clearing. The swaying pines provide a canopy of shade that gives the September air a bite. She presses down on the mulchy earth at the base of the mushroom, then slides it out of the ground. She drops the chanterelle into the basket and moves on to the next one.

'We're very lucky to find this,' Gert says. 'It's important we don't tell anyone.'

Tatiana pulls up another mushroom. She traces a finger over the ridges that run along the underside of its cap. Her gut spins with the thrill and guilt of keeping a secret. 'Isn't it better to share it?'

Gert stands up slowly. He takes off his fleece and wraps it around his waist in an attempt to conceal the dark patch on his jeans. 'No. They didn't show up. So now they will have to find their own *kantareller*.'

'What if they find the wrong ones, like I did?' Tatiana says, another mushroom plucked from the ground. 'You need to teach them what you know. Like you taught me.'

Gert thinks about this a moment. Memories arrange themselves before him: the waking thirst, empty space of Emil's seat, twenty years laced with lies. Before that: a hardback book of mycology, illustrated pages of gills, stems, spores. His father's volatile shame in fearing his son might know more about something than he did. Gert's boyhood wonder made hard and sharp, its softness given edges. 'It's bad to think you know everything.'

In her past life – a time that feels as distant as her childhood but in reality was a matter of months ago – the students at the university had looked to Tatiana as a knower of things. They had trusted her to know the locations and return dates of the books they wanted to borrow; sometimes, if a student was studying a subject Tatiana had come to know well, they might trust her recommendations of extra-curricular reading. Above all, Tatiana thought, the students had trusted her to stay silent when government officials demanded to know which of them had led recent organising efforts; if she'd seen them, which she undeniably had, hunched at one of the library's tables, speaking in urgent whispers. Sometimes, as she dusts the children's books in their reading corner, she wants to turn to the other women and tell them about the dark wood of the university library, the rich smell of its volumes, imprinted by the fingers of countless learners.

Gert finds a moss-covered stone to perch on where the clearing recedes into woodland, from where he watches Tatiana, the quick work of her fingers, a bushel's worth of mushrooms felled by her newly competent hands. The mid-afternoon sky swells, threatening rain. This, Gert knows, will be good for the crop, the moisture creating the perfect conditions for mushrooms to spread and grow throughout the forest. 'It's going to rain soon,' he says.

'Oh, yes. We should go back now,' Tatiana says, although she doesn't feel ready to leave. Here in the forest, with her hands in the overripe earth, her world feels simpler; no social faux pas to lose sleep overthinking, no migration office appointments. As they make their way back towards the car park, Tatiana remembers lunch breaks spent wandering amongst the ancient oak trees of the university's botanical gardens, gnarled branches knotting in the grey sky above her and age-old roots tangled below. She had been alone there, pinching the corners of her smoked ham sandwich, though she'd felt so very far from it.

Raindrops streak the windscreen of Gert's car. It's an old Volvo which once belonged to his father, and as she drives it, Tatiana can feel its unwieldiness. Driving used to make Tatiana feel powerful. Her licence, expired, sits at the back of the kitchen drawer with other forms of obsolete identification. She grips the steering wheel and stares straight down the road, to the scattering of red houses dotted across the field. Beside her in the passenger seat, Gert sifts through their bounty. 'You must always double check,' he says.

They drive past swathes of arable land. Dairy cows doze in

small clusters, so still that they look as though they've been carved from stone. Sometimes, Tatiana finds herself longing for the sour, earthbound smell of cows. She'd been back to her family farm only once, three months before her mother died. She'd begged Tatiana to go with her on the one weekend of the year when former residents were permitted to enter the zone without much supervision. Tatiana had watched from the car as her mother picked wildflowers from the paddock to lay against their front door. Within weeks, guide groups would once again be escorting tourists through the reserve, perhaps even past their old home; people who'd come from all over the world for a fleeting taste of well-marketed tragedy. As they approached the edge of the reserve, Tatiana felt her claim to the place she'd been born loosen. Scientists said the disaster had been good for the area. Wolf populations had thrived, and rare species of plants grew unhindered. In distant meadowland, Tatiana's mother was sure she spotted endangered wild horses, roaming their very own kingdom.

'You're a natural,' Gert says.

Tatiana gives him a momentary glance. 'I got my licence very young.'

He holds a chanterelle by the base of its fleshy stem. 'With the mushrooms.'

Tatiana feels her cheeks redden. Nothing about being here has come naturally to her; everywhere she goes, she feels as though she's breaking imaginary rules that no one has bothered to explain. The business of mushroom picking is one of few rules, needing only a basic knowledge of the edible varieties. A precise hand fixed to a pliable stem is all it takes for the weight of the bounty to pleasantly rise. With each chanterelle tossed into the basket, Tatiana had felt more like there could be a place for her here after all.

Gert had not expected to need to be driven home. As they pull into the driveway of his cottage, he feels a twinge of shame on account of its unruly appearance. One day, soon, he'll get to the peeling facade, strip away the rot and apply a fresh coat of paint. He'll pull up the dandelions in the garden by their roots and repair the crack that runs like a vein through the kitchen window. He'll speak to his doctor, too; about the fainting, and the way that he sometimes feels like a fist is closing tight across his chest. He has so much time, Gert thinks, an abundance of time during which he can do these things. In the car, with the basket of mushrooms in his lap, he feels hopeful.

They unload Tatiana's bike. With this detour, her distance home has doubled, a truth that sits thick in the humid air. 'I can take some mushrooms in here,' she says, unzipping her backpack.

'Yes, OK,' Gert says, but he doesn't lift the basket from its place on the ground between them. Instead, he says, 'They're very good eaten fresh.'

Tatiana does not want to leave. The thought shocks her in its sudden earnestness, catching in her throat like the threat of tears. She has always struggled with the temporary presence of strangers, that transitory bond that is severed as swiftly as it's formed. She wonders what she'll do with her half of the pickings; it would be indulgent, she thinks, to cook an elaborate dish for herself, no one with whom to enjoy it. She imagines herself stopping by the side of a quiet road and dumping the mushrooms into a ditch where wildflowers grow, a feast for the deer.

Gert's trousers are cool and stiff. He's desperate to change them. But he's thinking about the way golden chanterelles smell when sautéed in a thumb of butter, fresh garlic crushed on top. This, surely, is a smell of godly design; no human being could conceive of such a pleasing combination. It would be disrespectful, he thinks, to let the cottage fill with this heavenly scent, with no one but the cat as companion. 'If you have time,' he says to Tatiana, who he thinks might be crying, or about to, though he isn't sure why, 'I could cook them for us.'

Tatiana wipes at her cheeks with the back of her hand. Relief runs through her like an overflowing river. She thinks about radioactive dust raining down on both of their countries, settling deep in the ground to be absorbed into the mushrooms and berries, the bellies of the beasts that consume them. Through her tears, she smiles for the first time in months. 'I have time,' she says, wheeling her bike up the path and leaning it against the wall. 'I have time.'

# *Little Bird*

Piper's made a friend. I can tell she's trying to hide her excitement, but it slips through in the way she bites her lip and pulls at the frayed hem of her dress. 'She started at the fish market this week,' she says. 'She was born in Gibraltar, but her family moved here when she was six. Her name's Raquel.'

We're sitting on the edge of the swimming pool, dangling our legs into its waterless belly. The evening sun warms the cool brick walls and catches the fuzzy golden hairs we've missed on our shins. We're not the kind of girls to have friends. Mum says it's because we're not really from here, even though it's where we were born. Mum's never got used to the heat, how it stiffens the air in a room. She tells us about the purple moors she grew up on, the wind that swept through the heather. The heat is all we've known.

'I asked her if she wanted to go to La Palma on Saturday night,' Piper says.

I flinch. 'We've never been there.'

'No,' Piper says.

'Do you think Mum will mind?'

Piper kicks her heels against the side of the pool. 'You know she won't.'

In the low light, the wasteland looks like a graveyard. People's dreams have died here. None of the houses have windows, or doors; some don't even have walls. Property bust, recession, words we were too young to know the meaning of at the time. In the village, people talk about the wasteland's fabled inhabitant: a feral girl who howls like a wolf. Mum says not even the junkies feel safe here any more.

Mum has only one rule: don't go to the wasteland. We disobey this often, and without subtlety. But we heed her warning for what to do if we encounter the wolf girl. Told to us at an age when fear alchemised into permanent compliance in our young minds, it's the only thing that makes sense. Stand your ground, she said, and we'll never forget the horrible wideness of her eyes when she said it. Stand your ground and say your prayers. God will know what to do.

It's hard to imagine the presence of any god in the wasteland. Aside from the clusters of weeds that have broken through the paving stones in front of doorless thresholds, nothing grows here. Dust comes away on our hands as we rest sweaty palms on cinder blocks. It gets everywhere, this restless, clouding dirt; sloughing itself from the walls to be blinked into our eyes and collected on the straps of our sandals. In the corners of would-be homes we find the ghosts of other trespassers: spent needles and stained mattresses, a copy of *Lolita* with a hole burned through the cover. We push at these artefacts with careful toes, as though prodding at the bodies of dead birds. This is what we do in the wasteland: walk its shadowed paths, cataloguing what we see. We've never been to a museum, but we imagine they are something like this.

Mum likes the triptychs best, biblical passages painted in Renaissance style, encased in three carved wooden frames. She spends hours scrolling through websites to find the rarest pieces. These, she says, are the most popular, resulting in dozens of online bidders pushing up the price. Her mood follows the tides of triumph and loss. A winning bid, and she'll take us for pizza at the beach, or give us an extra euro each to spend at the bakery on the corner. A loss will be weathered in silence, her bedroom door closed.

It is because of a string of losses that she hasn't yet realised I've stopped going to school for the most part, weeks before schedule. Instead I follow Piper to the market and watch her put dead fish on ice, her gloved hands arranging their slippery bodies. She says you get used to the smell, to the sound of oysters cracking open. It's the eyes I can't bear, open even in death, like the glazed beads of a rosary chain.

I sit on a folding chair just outside the market and flick through the pages of a guide to 'offgrid living' in Alaska. I've become skilled at lifting magazines from the shelves of the kiosk in the village, Piper distracting the proprietor with some pointless question about the price of a stick of gum. I skip the boring bits about permits and power generation to read about farming a small plot of land for food. In the cool aisles of the market, Piper and her colleagues gut fish while the customers wait, looking down. They don't want to feel the loosening of flesh under a knife or clear the spooling intestines away.

Later, we walk to the wasteland; slow, heavy footsteps, sandals slapping against the pavement. Heat liquifies under our arms and between our shoulder blades. 'Do you miss school?' Piper asks.

On the cracked asphalt playground, girls would sit in circles and force down laughter as I went past, the meaner ones shouting 'Where's your weird sister?' or 'Piper Pescado, *aletas al lado*,' sucking their cheeks in to imitate the puckered lips of a fish out of water. I kick a pebble out of my path. 'No.'

Filth has gathered in the corners of the empty pool. Sometimes, we guess at what it might be: mulched leaves, though there are no trees nearby; rotten grout seeping out from between tiles. We daren't go down there; we've no way of knowing we'd be able to safely emerge. The ladder was stripped away by metal thieves long before we first came here, and even at the shallower end, the curve of the wall doesn't lend itself to climbing. Instead, we play at swimming through the thick, hot air, bending our arms and puffing out our chests. We have to, it's too sad if we don't; too sad to think of an open wound in the ground, never tended.

Piper rests her head on my shoulder and lays her arm across my lap, taut skin of her wrist like the underbelly of some amphibious creature. 'Please, Little Bird?'

I hesitate only a moment before lifting my hand over her outstretched arm. My fingers come to rest on her skin, to drift back and forth like a feather.

Saturday comes, and we don't know what to do with ourselves. We wake early after barely any sleep, eat our bowls of cereal on the sofa with the sunrise. Piper is used to dawn, those hours when every sound – a barking dog on its morning walk, the crunch of slow tyres on the street below our building – carries amplified weight. She switches on the TV, low volume so as not to disturb Mum, flicking to the garish colours of the cartoons we used to watch when we were younger.

I'm just slipping back into sleep when Piper sits bolt upright on the sofa. 'Let's practise ordering drinks.'

'Do you think we need to? We've ordered things before.' I shift away from her on the sofa. 'We buy things all the time at the bakery.'

'Yeah, but this is different, Little Bird,' Piper says, breath milk-sour. 'We're talking about ordering drinks. At a bar.'

I look across the room to the glass display cabinet which houses Mum's triptychs and relics. Dust gathers slowly up here on the ninth floor but she cleans it every weekend anyway, taking every piece out and pushing a damp cloth between the folds in the wood. 'Mum might hear us,' I say.

'Just,' she says, pushing mouse-brown baby hairs away from her face. She smiles, takes a deep breath. '*Me gustaría una Coca-Cola, por favor.*'

I fall back on the sofa, groaning, and cover my face with my hands.

'What?' Piper says, tugging at my wrists.

'It's just . . . you don't sound like you,' I say.

'That's the whole point,' she says. 'Tonight, we can be whoever we want to be.'

So, we take it in turns. We jut out our chins, arch back our shoulders, try to add years to our voices. We play with different orders – piña colada for Piper, virgin mojito for me – dissolving into giggles. We're nervous. We sound like children. We're not the kind of girls to have friends.

Raquel arrives at La Palma two minutes late. We stir the ice cubes in our tall glasses of Coke and watch her negotiate a path across the sand, order a drink at the bar. Piper leans forward, splaying her fingers across the shiny, black surface of the hydraulic bar table we're sitting at. I know the type of table it is because it's very popular in bars like this one, or so says the industry brochure I read outside the market on one of Piper's recent shifts. 'See how she does it?' she says, kicking my shin.

I fiddle with the strands of hair that have fallen loose from my ponytail and stuck themselves against the side of my neck. Piper spears the thin slice of lemon in her glass with the end of her straw, sending fragments of sour pulp afloat. 'She must have had more practice than we've had,' she says.

Raquel is wearing a denim skirt. Her butterscotch hair is held back from her face by a giant clip in the shape of a conch shell. It's a style I recognise from a fashion magazine I swiped from the kiosk last month. As she gets closer, I see that the tops of her cheeks are pink with sunburn.

'*Hola chicas,*' she says, sitting down at our table. Her voice is flat and gravelly.

'Are you sick?' Piper asks.

Raquel draws her face back, sinking her chin into her neck. 'What? No.'

'Your voice,' Piper says, pointing at her own throat. 'You sound like you might be sick.'

Raquel looks briefly towards the bar, then opens the tiny denim handbag on her lap and produces a hip flask. I've seen such things before, lifted from the pockets of unstable detectives in the noir films we watch on Sunday afternoons. The surface of the flask is dull against Raquel's pointed, acid-green nails. 'This is just how I sound,' she says, unscrewing the lid. She doesn't seem offended. 'Too many cigarettes, maybe.'

Piper is frowning at the flask, working her tongue into the gap next to her canine tooth. 'What's that?'

'Drink like half of your Cokes, quickly,' Raquel says, pinching her straw.

I look at Piper, brow still knotted, then back at Raquel, whose eyes look like they're bulging; waiting, expectant. A sound comes from Piper, the fleshing of a question, cut short by me closing my mouth around the straw and siphoning the Coke up and away. The carbonated liquid stings at the bridge of my nose, coating my teeth in a syrupy film. The straw twirls away as I part my lips and wait for Piper's wrath. She stares at me, stone-faced, the giveaway flare of her nostrils perceptible only if you know to look for it. Then, she plucks her own straw between tight fingers, the level of the Coke sinking quickly as she sucks in her cheeks.

Once Piper's done, we lift our heads from our glasses and watch, entranced, as Raquel pours a clear substance into each drink. Then, she slips the flask back into her bag, smooths a hand over the wave of her hair. 'My dad makes his own vodka, brews it, or whatever. He never notices when I dip into his stash.'

'Right,' Piper says. Her voice rings with forced admiration. It's a trick we would never have thought of during our hours of practice this morning.

We sit in silence, stirring our drinks and looking around the bar. The barman is watching a muted football match on the screen hooked up to the metal frame, distractedly dragging a cloth across the taps every now and again. At the table underneath the screen, an old man is swivelling a napkin with routine jabs of his finger. Above the shhh, shhh of the waves, tinny music plays out of the speakers. We don't know the song; of course we don't. Raquel might, though, and I'm about to ask her when Piper slips down from her stool. 'I want to dance.'

Raquel lets out a snort. 'OK.'

'Don't you want to?' Piper says.

Raquel looks at me, as if I might know what to say, then back to Piper. 'There's no one here.'

Piper has begun to sway. 'You never dance alone?'

'It's just that there's not even really a dance floor, and no one else is dancing. It's early.'

In the circle of space between the bar and the table where the man sits with his swivelling napkin, Piper curls her arms in and out of the sides of her waist. Under her white linen dress, she juts sharp hip bones left and right, keeping her legs rooted in place. The beat of the song moves quicker than she does, unnatural sounds demanding things of her body she doesn't want to give. The barman gives her only a cursory glance before returning his attention to the football, a slow cloth moving over the rim of a glass perhaps more times than is necessary. I feel my face burning. I can't look at her any longer. Instead I look at Raquel, tapping her nails against the side of her glass, eyes roaming with restless unease.

'These tables are powered by hydraulics,' I say. The sound of my own voice shocks me.

Raquel keeps tapping. 'Oh really.'

On the shore a stone's throw away, a group of girls are walking through the foam left behind by the waves. They're cackling, howling with laughter; tanned limbs luminescent in the sunset.

'Have you ever been to the wasteland?' I say.

Her fingers still. 'No. Why? Have you?'

'We could take you.'

Raquel takes a deep breath in. She looks around the near-empty bar, and at Piper, still moving in slow, fluid motions. 'Yeah, OK.'

We drain our glasses, slide down from our stools. When we reach Piper, I place a hand on her arm. 'Where are you going?' she asks.

'I thought we could show Raquel the wasteland.'

Straight away, I realise I've made a mistake. We've never taken anyone there, never spoken of it to others. Piper's face clouds with the pain of betrayal, but underneath: a glimpse of something else. 'Sure.'

On languid days at the fish market, or evenings throwing stones against the paper-thin walls of the wasteland, or mornings circling the closed door of the bakery, I think about our grandmother, whose nickname I was given at birth. Dolores, Mum says of her one-time mother-in-law, was the daughter of a hunter; a sweet-natured woman with a gentle heart and an unmatched ability to anticipate the feelings of others. Her father called her his 'little bird,' his Birdie; she was always running off, out of sight, a migratory bird. Her singing would greet him when he arrived home from hunting or trapping. He'd trapped Iberian wolves, before the regulations, used their furs to keep his family warm in the unforgiving mountains. This is how I imagine her: a bird in the skin of a wolf, wearing the legacy of a beast much more fearsome than she was.

I tell Raquel this story as we walk towards the wasteland. Every sound of acknowledgement she makes sends a thrill through my stomach, because my voice, my words, being the focus of someone's attention is new and exciting. Even as I sense her interest waning, I keep talking, gorging myself on forbidden joy that could be snatched away at any moment. Ahead of us, Piper walks quickly, sandals scuffing the bone-dry pavement. She's walking with her arms crossed, something Mum has always warned us against. I'm about to remind her of this when Raquel presses her bare arm into mine. The lid of the hip flask glints.

'Your *abuela* sounds like the wolf girl,' Raquel says, wincing as she takes a sip. 'I heard she survives by killing birds with stones and eating them raw.'

I take the flask, bring it to my lips. The vodka tastes chemical, like the smell of bleach; I shrink at how childish this reaction makes me feel, take another gulp for good measure. The borders of my senses start to blur. I pass the flask back to Raquel. 'I heard she even eats the feathers.'

We're at the edge of town now, the path inclining upwards. The wasteland peeks out between barren hills, moonlight looming on its crumbling walls. As we ascend the height of the path and walk through the gap where the gate had been stripped, I think of Mum's glass cabinet, how proudly she displays the spoils of her biddings. I feel strangely wide open; I want to take Raquel's hand and lead her through the rooms of this place, show her its ancient histories. We've never thought of it as anyone's but ours.

A clicking sound, when we reach the pool; a spark of light at Raquel's lips, embers dropped to the dirt floor. She exhales, tilts the box towards Piper.

In the fleeting motion of Piper's head turning towards me, Raquel sees it. 'Oh my god, you've never smoked before?' There's a bite to her voice that reminds me of the girls at school, sitting on their jackets on the blistering tarmac.

Piper snatches at the packet, scrambling when the cigarettes slide out onto the ground. I feel like I should help but I find myself rooted in place, watching her ponytail fall over her shoulder as she stoops to collect them. Raquel's laugh glitters with cruelty, but it sounds like a form of acceptance, and isn't this what we've longed for: the fickle interests of girls we can only dream of becoming? This, I suppose, is a friendship: birds and wolves learning to live with each other.

'Here,' Raquel says, pulling at Piper's arm until their heads are a handspan apart. 'Put it in your mouth.' Piper does as she's told, and Raquel leans towards her, the ends of their cigarettes touching until Piper's flickers into light.

I toe the edge of the pool, the cracked flagstones laid there years ago by men with uncertain futures ahead of them. I smell of sweat and mosquito repellent, the thick sun cream smoothed onto the back of my neck by Piper this afternoon. Sinking down to her haunches, Piper coughs and wretches, throwing the cigarette into the pool. 'Let's play a game,' she says once she recovers, looking up at me. 'What do you say, Little Bird?'

Sudden goosebumps appear on my arms. I think of Mum's wide eyes: *Stand your ground and say your prayers*. My voice is almost a whisper. 'Should we? Raquel might not like—'

'Raquel wants to play,' Raquel says, smudging her cigarette out on the ground. I notice she wears the same colour polish on her toenails; acid-green against the thin, tall wedge of her espadrilles.

Piper moves quickly, dust kicked up by the rush of her running away. Raquel steps back. 'What the—'

'Run!' I tell her, and I slip through my own labyrinth, skin snagging on rotting walls.

The game is always the same: we split from each other, hide in the hollowed-out shells of the wasteland's empty houses, and howl. We've found ways to make ourselves louder, made instruments out of discarded metal pans and sheets of corrugated iron. Our voices shapeshift across the dry, broken structures, bouncing towards and away from one another. We can't always tell which howl belongs to who, or which of us is telling the truth when we claim to have stopped long before the howling ended. It's a question that both scares and thrills us, one that only the wasteland can answer.

So, I do as I always do. I round the corner into the darkened husk of what might have been a hallway or kitchen, duck down against the rough wall by a glassless window and howl. I turn my face upwards, stretch my throat, bring the sound up from the pit of my lungs. I feel like we alone are meant to do this; I feel alive with the rightness of it, the way every howl melts my fears and uncertainties away. I think of Dolores; how, to the right ears, a wolf's howl might sound a lot like birdsong.

And then I hear it: a scream, sharp and short against the dead air.

We're out of breath when we reach the pool, adrenaline making our heads spin. 'Did you hear that?' Piper says, and I nod. 'Do you think . . . ?' she says, and I'm not sure what she means, but again I nod my head.

We straighten our dresses, scratch at new bites on our arms. We don't want to look, though we know we have to, know we will. I've never seen Piper like this before. The ground feels unsteady beneath me, like liquid, like the world is upside down. I feel Piper's hand slip into mine and move me closer to the edge of the pool, until we are right beside it and can look nowhere else but into its waterless depths. Piper's hand slackens in mine; a flood of relief – Raquel isn't there. We nearly miss it in the darkness, but I catch its pearlescent glow: the conch shell, a thin crack through the surface like a strand of mermaid's hair.

\*

Time turns elastic while I wait for Piper on my chair outside the market. I skim the pages of an in-flight magazine I found abandoned on the beach, but the words seem to shrink as I read them. 'I was wrong to make a friend,' Piper had said last night as we walked home from the wasteland, shivering with something other than cold after an hour spent pointlessly searching its darkest corners. I'd felt the tears coming then, and had turned my face away from her. It seemed fated to end up like this, but still, we had let ourselves hope.

Deep into the long afternoon, Piper emerges. Her pale skin glimmers in the sunlight, and for a second I imagine her sea-bound, arms slick with scales. 'She didn't come in,' she says. As if sensing my fear, she adds, 'But I'm sure she will tomorrow.'

I have never doubted my sister, always taken her word as truth. Imagining a version of reality where it's not safe to trust what she says does something strange to me, unsettling the normal functions that keep me anchored in myself. I know she's not sure. I know this clearly, with force. The strange thing is happening inside me: a quickening of my blood, a hardening of the soft skin I've always lived in.

At home, we heat frozen pizzas in the oven and dip the slices into a jar of mayonnaise. Mum's door is closed but behind it we can hear the plastic click of the mouse. The glass cabinet looms like a third child in the corner while we lick melted cheese off our fingers, retrieve discs of pepperoni from the floor. We watch badly dubbed movies, the room darkening around us until only the artificial glow of the TV remains.

I wait until Piper's asleep before I slip on my sandals and close the door to the apartment as gently as I can behind me. Outside, there's a bite to the air that reminds me the season will change soon. Piper will start to look for work elsewhere, somewhere warmer, away from the water; the school term will begin again. I don't know what I'll do. I don't know anything, except that I'm heading for the wasteland; searching for ghosts, old and new.

I stand by the side of the pool, the late summer breeze cool on my skin. I lift my foot to see the crushed cigarette butt on the flagstone, another nestled in the grime in the corner of the pool. I grimace with the memory of Piper coughing and spluttering; it had hurt to see her try to be someone else, a splitting ache as she tried to break away. Where the tiles decline at the deep end: Raquel's conch shell hair clip. It's part of the fabric of this place now, a missed stitch in the seam.

What I should do comes to me then, not from my own mind, but from hers, because it's what Birdie would do, wings beating under the hide. So I take myself inside, strain my neck and open my mouth, and wait for sound to come out.

# *Foxglove*

We stop halfway there to go to the supermarket. We buy still-warm sourdough rolls, avocados that dimple when we press them. Basil and pine nuts for pesto we'll make at the weekend, unwaxed lemons, two bulbous heads of garlic. Seb wheels the trolley down aisle after aisle and I follow, gripping Ellie's hand. She pulls against my hold, desperate to slip out and away, so she might run past her father and disappear around the corner. I tighten my grip.

We walk back to the car, the wind whipping our hair. Ellie walks quickly, eager to return to her games on the back seat. I do not let go of her hand.

It took us an hour to find her, sixty minutes that felt like much longer. Now that Seb has turned it into a dinner-party anecdote, the length of time she was gone for has been reframed as a minor detail, a wave of the hand, a 'half an hour, give or take'. He never meets my eye when he shares these retellings.

The drive from the supermarket to the summer house is slow and silent. On stretches of clear, smooth road, Seb puts a hand on my knee. I feel the weight of his palm against my skin. I'm sure he's not thinking, like I am, about every one of those sixty minutes, this time and place last year. I shift in my seat so his hand moves away. In the rearview mirror, Ellie's head is bowed in concentration, fingers moving at lightspeed over the surface of her tablet.

The first thing we see when approaching the house is the foxgloves. They grow by the wooden rail of the veranda, gaping mouths in various shades of pink. Last year, Ellie – who, at seven, stands just a head above the tallest stems – put a finger into one of the flowers. I shouted, startling her away. Now, I imagine a whispered welcome slipping from their tongues like poison.

Seb pulls into the driveway. The foxgloves sway in the breeze and I try not to look.

In bed the next morning, my husband spills hot breath onto the tender skin at my neck. I twist away, but he's close behind. He puts a hand across my hip, his wedding ring glinting in the milky light.

'We should get rid of the foxgloves,' I say.

His body stiffens. The hand that has started to thumb at my thigh recedes.

My voice is cracked and low. 'They could poison Ellie.'

'Only if she eats a whole field of them,' Seb answers, rolling onto his back.

There's the sound of the door handle, and our daughter appears with a paper fortune teller in her upturned palms. Seb adjusts the covers, sits up against the headboard. 'It's barely six o'clock, El.'

Ellie jumps onto the end of the bed. 'Want me to tell you your future?'

She places one thumb then another, one index finger then the other, under the tips of the folded contraption, and begins to move her hands.

Later, I lay the table for breakfast. Ellie's future, as she had read it, will include freshly baked croissants, so Seb has gone down to the village to buy some. I prepare coffee, and warm milk for Ellie, who is flicking the fortune teller across the table, jumping down from her seat to retrieve it. There's a rush of pink in the corner of my vision as the foxgloves bob against the window. I could do it now, I think. I could take a knife to their stalks, bury their heads for the earth to gorge on.

We returned to the house after searching the woods for half an hour. It was brazen in its obliviousness, offering warmth and comfort as if we weren't hollow with panic. I wanted to laugh. I wanted to put my face into the cushions and scream. Instead, I went back to Ellie's room, begged for clues. There was her bed, unmade, sheet trailing on the floor. The folded pyjamas neatly stacked on her pillow, a heart-wrenching sign of obedience. There must be something I'm not seeing, I thought. There must be something else on which we can place the blame.

I went back into the living room. Seb was leaning against the breakfast bar, gnawing the skin at his thumb. 'We have to call the police,' I said.

He lowered his hand. 'And say what? How would we explain this?'

'It doesn't matter. We can just tell them what happened.'

When he didn't reply, I marched into the kitchen and ripped

the list of numbers off the fridge. As I reached for the phone in its cradle, Seb grabbed it and held it behind his back. 'We'll find her, Mara. She has to be somewhere.'

I looked at the empty cradle, the crumpled list of numbers in my hand, the bunch of bananas turning brown in their bowl. I looked at anything but my husband. 'She's not a fucking remote control stuck down the back of the sofa, Seb.'

His fist came down on the bar, the phone clattering to the floor. 'You think I don't know that?'

Tears clouded my sight. 'We have to report her missing.'

I brought myself to look at him then, this man that I loved. This man, who'd taken me camping and asked me to marry him as we toasted marshmallows over open flames with our four-year-old daughter. This man, who'd washed my hair and rubbed soap into my skin the day we found out that the child before Ellie would never say their first word, take a first step, or know this world at all.

Seb snatched the keys from the bar. 'She has to be somewhere.'

We walk down to the seafront in the afternoon. The coast bends away from us like a curved bow, and we point out boats in the distance, the arched wings of seagulls cawing above us. Seb and I sit down on a towel by the dunes, while Ellie pulls off her oversized t-shirt and runs towards the water. Except for a father and son coaxing a kite into flight by the rocks, we have the beach to ourselves.

I dig my toes into the sand and watch Ellie chase the tide, holding on to her sunhat. Seb unscrews the canteen he's brought, pours white wine into plastic cups. When he touches his hand to my arm to offer me a cup, I flinch. 'Sorry,' I say. 'I'm just tired.'

He strokes the back of my neck, moves my hair to the side. 'Maybe we can have an early night.'

Ellie is sitting in the shallows, splashing her hands in the water. 'Maybe.'

Seb leans back on the towel. His voice is small against the wide-open space, as if it has come from the mouth of a shell I hold to my ear. 'I don't know what you want me to do, Mara.'

The late-August sun is weak behind clouds. It's not a question, so I offer no reply. It's a statement, a confession. I rub my goose-bumped skin, pull the hem of my dress down to my ankles.

'You have to forgive yourself,' he says. 'I can't do it for you.'

I watch my daughter shovel sand into piles that, in her imagination, are mountains, or castles.

It was our fault that Ellie went missing. She'd wanted to explore the woods around the house, but we'd put her off with lukewarm promises of going out later instead. We'd given her paper and crayons, and left her outside, alone.

I remember my mouth pressed to Seb's, his hand under my skirt, the dull ache of the kitchen counter digging into my back. It had been so long. Outside, I could hear the wind whistling through the birch trees. Nothing mattered more to me in that moment. Then, I remember the crayons, rolled away; sheets of paper blown across the veranda. Running from room to room, clinging to doorways; certain there was a corner I hadn't checked, a stone left unturned.

For months afterwards, I'd sit on the toilet back home and pinch the skin at my inner thigh until I cried from the pain. Sixty pinches, one for every minute she'd been lost, felt like repentance. Then I'd climb into bed with my husband and wait, in vain, for him to speak.

*

When I wake up the next morning, Seb's side of the bed is empty. I check the pillow for warmth that might tell me how long he's been up and it's cool to the touch. Daylight streams through a crack in the curtains, soaking the room in stillness. I press my phone to life and the screen shows that it's gone eleven.

Sleep is a function I've come to view as selfish indulgence. I mimic my daughter's circadian rhythm as closely as I can; going to bed only when I'm sure she's asleep, waking up at least an hour before she does. Her routine has been harder to maintain during the school holidays, but I tell myself this disturbance, and the exhaustion it brings, is a suitable penance.

Through the slightly open door, I smell butter and smoke. I hear the frying pan crackling with heat and Ellie saying, 'Can I flip one?'

'The pan's too heavy for you, grub,' Seb replies.

Ellie jumps down from her seat at the table when I walk through. She runs to me, buries her head in my stomach. 'We're making you breakfast because you're tired,' she says, her hair matted and wild.

I bend to kiss the top of her head, breathe the scent of her into my lungs. She looks up at me, face glimmering with expectation. That's when I see it: the milk jug in the middle of the table, pink mouths open.

Ellie runs back to her seat and Seb comes over. I stare at the pancake batter bubbling on the stove. 'We've got maple syrup or lemon and sugar, your choice,' he says, slipping an arm around my waist. When I don't respond, he follows my line of sight to the flowers. 'Ellie helped me pick them.'

I jerk away from him, smile at Ellie who's looking up at us, confused. 'But, you know . . .' I say, tears prickling behind my eyes.

'You know I don't like them.'

Seb goes back to the pan, scrapes the overdone pancake into the sink. 'Ellie, what are those pretty flowers for?' he says.

Ellie slumps in her chair. 'Looking at.'

'And what are they not for?'

She stifles a laugh. 'Eating!'

I sit down next to Ellie. She traces invisible letters on the surface of her plate and I try to guess the distance between her hands and the flowers.

We found our child huddled in the hollow of a fallen tree, half a mile from the house. The sky was streaked orange, everything bathed in twilight splendour. I pawed at her limbs in silence, searching for wounds. 'You're hurting me, Mummy!' she shouted. The miracle of her unscathed skin left me breathless.

'We called for you, Ellie,' Seb said, his voice straining. 'We called your name over and over. Why didn't you answer?'

I pulled her small body to mine, breathed in the smell of her hair. I could feel my heart racing between us, beating for two.

'I was scared you'd be angry with me,' she sobbed.

I sunk to the ground, rocked my daughter back and forth in my lap until there was a bite to the air and no more orange sky.

Ellie demands another beach day, so we abandon a half-hearted game of Guess Who and walk down. It's Saturday, and the beach is crowded with families; we weave through a minefield of wilting parasols and rusting loungers, laying our towel down on a spot by the rocks. I grab Ellie's wrist as she turns to head for the water. 'Sunhat please,' I say, straightening the cotton rim across her forehead.

'It's like some sort of hellish Renaissance painting,' Seb says, nodding at the mass of children playing in the shallows. Despite myself, I feel the pull of a smile.

We sit in silence, watching Ellie bring handfuls of silt out of the water and letting it run, glistening, through her fingers. Older children push each other over behind her, the water rising in spurts as their backs break the surface. The air rings with the sound of their screams.

'All right,' Seb says, standing up. 'How about ice cream?'

Before I can answer, he's picking his way towards the truck in the dunes.

Next to me, a mother urges her child to stand still as she attempts to rub sunscreen onto their back. There's a tussle, and I feel small hands tug at my hair as the child topples into my lap.

'Amelia, apologise to that lady right now,' the mother says.

I look at them and smile. 'It's OK.'

When I turn back around, I can no longer see my daughter in the shallows. There is just the yellow crown of her sunhat bobbing in the water.

Everything but that hat – the mother, the sunscreen, the bent spine of a splayed book I step on – blurs at the edge of my vision as I sprint towards the water. I hear myself calling her name. The fear is physical, primal; the only real thing. Then I'm in the water, far beyond the children, slicing through gentle waves towards the thin line of the horizon.

A chorus of voices, like sirens, call to me from the shore. Seb, an ice cream in each hand, Ellie by his side.

I walk ahead of them on the way home, my spent limbs burning with every uphill step. When their shadows stretch out in front of me, I up my pace. By the time we reach the house, I am breathless with exertion. I stare at the foxgloves, the patch of mutilated stumps, the gardening gloves Seb has left there.

Ellie kicks off her shoes at the door before going to her room. I walk back and forth in the kitchen, watch Seb put the game of Guess Who away, folding each plastic flap down with care. 'I thought she'd drowned.'

Seb slides the lid cleanly over its box and leans back on the sofa. 'Is it not far more likely that she saw me going for ice cream and followed me out to the truck, which is exactly what happened?'

I think of the sunhat floating at the water's edge. My voice is a knife. 'I looked away for a second and when I turned around she was gone.'

'She knows not to go more than ankle deep, Mara,' he says. 'You need to learn to trust her.'

'Why didn't you call the police, Seb?' I spit.

He looks at me, confused. 'Because I knew where she was.'

'No,' I say. 'Before.'

The space between us spoils like rotten fruit. I stare at him slouched on the sofa, jaw clenched, eyes down. 'Because calling would have made it real, and I couldn't make it real,' he says, choking back tears.

The sudden smallness of his voice takes me back to the last time I saw my husband cry. The gel, cold on my skin; indecipherable shapes on the screen. The nurse's fading smile as she went to get the doctor. He'd held my hand in his and tried to hide his fear. It's OK, he'd kept saying. It's OK. He'd kept hold of my hand and together we'd listened to the sound of car horns beeping outside while we waited for the nurse to come back.

*

We drive home the following day, stop at the supermarket halfway. Ellie strolls down the aisles, brushing her fingers against the shelves. We buy biscuits, cartons of juice; bottled water and napkins. As we make our way outside, Ellie slips between parked cars, waiting, crouched behind bonnets, for her father to find her. I listen for the sound of her laughter, plimsolls on the tarmac.

As night paints the sky pastel pink, Seb takes my hand in his. He smooths his thumb over my skin, gives a gentle squeeze. I sense him glance in my direction, but I don't turn to face him. Instead, I watch the trees blur past outside, delighting in the movement of wheels against road that is taking us forward.

# Tools for Surviving a Storm

Hours before Lewis blew his head off with his pistol, we made love in the old coble. It was warm for September, with a warning breeze that seemed to be telling us something. It was a ridiculous place to make love. Smell of rotten fish that you could never quite scrub away. The hull was rough against my buttocks, and though the cove we'd sailed to was empty, whether or not it'd stay that way was anyone's guess. Risk had always enticed Lewis's appetite. That Christine Howard and her righteous gaggle of beach cleaners could turn up on the shore any moment only made him more eager. As, I suppose, did the fact that he knew this would be the last time.

I'd have liked to have been in on that. Didn't seem fair, seeing as it was something I'd worried about for years. There was always going to be a last time. I'd expected it to be before we were both in our seventies, but sex was like a pair of fine leather shoes: better the older we got. It was the forgetting what'd do it, I thought. Happen the pistol saw to it first.

The rain comes a week after the funeral. Barely a shower at first, then more than you know what to do with. In my housecoat, I string a sheet of tarpaulin from the trellis on the garden wall to cover the flowerbeds. I can take a beating from the heavens, but the hydrangeas are far too soft. Inside, I hang my coat on the door to dry and watch the water run off the edge of the sheet onto the lawn. Everyone's in a flap about the weather. It started when those men came down from the fancy university, with their laser readings and erosion predictions and whatever else. And then there was the landslip earlier in the year, claimed a chunk of the cliff path. That likely hadn't helped.

Lewis hadn't given it a minute's grace. 'You ask me, it's a whole lot of bother over nowt.' He'd never feared the elements. He'd earned his badge of honour twenty years earlier, when a freak storm had blown in from Scandinavia and flipped the coble upside down like a penny. He'd lost the afternoon's catch and spent the night at Whitby hospital recovering from a touch of hypothermia. Nothing he wouldn't laugh off days later over a pint with young Danny Collins, who'd been on his first shift with the coastguard that night and was as shaken as if it'd been him who'd spent an hour clinging to the side of a capsized boat.

I sit in the conservatory and watch the hydrangeas bow in the wind. They say coastal erosion is gradual. Bad weather bites at the cliff side, chewing it up a little at a time until a great hunk falls away. The forgetting happened like that. Fumbling over which numbers to play on the lottery, having picked the same ones for ten years. Tying himself in knots trying to tell me the simplest of stories. One night,

I woke to him scrambling through the dresser for his oilskin jacket. His back was silver in the moonlight. 'Make me a bacon butty will you, love? I've got to get a move on or the boys'll leave without me,' he said. I hadn't the heart to tell him. He came down to the kitchen ten minutes later and couldn't for the life of him understand what'd compelled me to cook breakfast at four in the morning.

Lewis wasn't one for half-measures. Take the coast all at once, none of this little-by-little, easy-does-it destruction. A pistol was a landslip. Life fell away, quick as a flash. He did it in the evening, feigning a trip to the offie. He groaned as he knelt down to tie his shoelaces, joking about the afternoon's labour. 'Bye, love,' he said, by the door. I hadn't looked up from my ironing. He walked to the cordoned-off cliff path and called Sergeant Dale Dorsey, who he knew would arrive too late.

Christine Howard takes her tea with a sprinkle of sugar. Not a teaspoon or a pinch but a sprinkle. To indicate this she holds her hand up and rubs her fingers together in a flourish. She's sitting on the very edge of the settee, bony knees clasped together. Next to her, Emily Dorsey looks flighty, like she's ready to bolt any second. 'Milk and two sugars please, Franny.'

The neighbours all left this morning. I watched through the front-room window as Dale Dorsey and his boys took their suitcases and herded them onto the idling minibus. Well, I wasn't going to be ferried two-by-two onto Noah's Ark to sit up all night on a camping bed in the village hall. By the time the sergeant knocked at the door, I'd already backed into the conservatory. His voice was faint as a ghost's through the letterbox. 'Enough of this now, Franny, it's not what Lewis would've wanted.'

Emily Dorsey parrots her husband's words as she sips her brew.

'I twisted Dale's arm to come and talk some sense into you, Franny. But if you won't listen to reason then will you not think of Lewis? He'd want you to survive this.'

Christine puts a slender hand on Emily's arm. 'We all want you to survive this. We're still holding out hope that you'll come back to bridge club. We've never had such a challenging opponent!'

'I'm not budging,' I say, putting my tea cup down with a clatter. 'And if you think you can tempt me with an open return to the bridge club, which, by the way, I was relieved to be shot of, then you've got another thing coming.'

The wind rails against the window, howling like a beast in the chimney breast. Emily jerks her head towards the street. 'This isn't working, Christine. Let's go while we still can.'

'What do you think's going to happen, Emily?' I say, standing up. 'Ground's going to give way beneath us, is it? Holbeck Hall sliding into the sea live on't evening news?'

'Yes, Franny, that's exactly what I think, and I don't much fancy being here for it.' She gathers her coat from the arm of the settee. 'Christine, let's go.'

'Franny,' Christine says, taking my hands. Her skin is clammy, as though it's soaked up some of the downpour. She smiles. 'You either come with us now or you'll be dragged out of here kicking and screaming.'

I yank my hands away. 'Threaten me all you like. I'm staying put.'

The front door slams, and we watch Emily's umbrella fold like a cowardly spy under the pressure of the horizontal rain. 'Forecast isn't bad enough for them to force me out of here, Christine. You know that. Ground feels solid to me.'

Christine Howard doesn't easily admit defeat. She petitions

the council over just about anything you can think of, and emerges victorious more often than not. The strength it takes for her to put on her raincoat and bow her head in concession isn't to be sniffed at. 'Stubborn as an old boot, you are,' Lewis always told me. An old boot that could weather any storm, and will certainly sail through this one.

When a man blows his head off with a pistol, the birds don't sing a song for mourning. No. The neighbour's cat stretches on the garden wall while the distant shot rings out. The sky doesn't darken in grief. His wife is none the wiser. She presses out creases in a shirt he'll never wear again. The rain pours, wetting the soil that covers his coffin, undermining the structural integrity of the house he shared with his childhood sweetheart. Nothing will ever be the same but the earth keeps turning.

Nature didn't much care when Lewis started forgetting, either. The day he lost his way to The Cod, the seagulls circled above it like they always had and always would. The sea had laid claim to that too, during the Great Storm of 1953; washed it clean into the waves. The pub had been rebuilt. But nothing could be done about the forgetting. It would keep whittling away at him until it'd worked him down to the quick.

When Sergeant Dorsey turned up with his hat in his hands, the sunset was golden on the water. I knew straight away why Lewis had done it. That day on the way to The Cod, he'd turned away from me in the street. 'Weren't in't mood for a drink anyroad,' he'd said. We'd never discussed it. His father had gone the same way, a gradual forgetting that sucked every penny they had into residential care. He'd die before he took me for a stranger or left me struggling to make ends meet. A pistol was a landslip. Quick, painless. Now, when I think about him doing it, I picture the missing cliff path and the old police cordon billowing in the wind as he squeezed on the trigger.

Tools for surviving a storm: torchlight, batteries, candles and matches. Stock up on tea bags, biscuits, powdered milk. Have lots of hope, you'll need it. Especially when the power goes out. Know how to get a fire going. Think of happy memories: picking blackberries in your grandmother's garden; running down to the harbour of an afternoon to watch the cobles wash in from the sea. Lewis, on that last day, hitching your dress up to your hips like a teenager. Don't think about what might have been if only you'd talked things through.

By evening, rain is lashing sideways at the windows. The sea is roaring something rotten, bellowing into the breakwaters. I stand in the conservatory and let the noise swallow me. It sounds like a gunshot might if you slowed it right down. It feels like the wind could shatter the glass like a bullet. In the garden, the hydrangeas hold on under their makeshift shelter. The stone wall stands its ground, as does the soft cliff below it. The house will not be breached.

I eat cream crackers and cheese for tea. I cut chunks of cheddar away from the block and think about the night the Scandinavian storm left Lewis bobbing about in the waves. I'd begged the sea to spare him as I watched Danny Collins and the coastguard sail out. But I knew nature to be merciless. It hadn't let him live out of kindness, and it didn't care a jot if the house fell into the sea. People turn to God for protection from natural disasters. A prayer a day won't stop an earthquake from destroying your house and killing your husband, but divine intervention means you're destined to escape with your life. If you ask me, there's a perfect calm to be found in knowing just how powerless you are. I look for that calm as I eat my crackers in the front room. I run towards it as I listen to the windows creak in their frames and the fishing boats break against the harbour.

I'd been a coward to pretend the forgetting wasn't happening. While the lucid days outnumbered the bad ones, it'd been easier to keep my mouth shut. I wouldn't have known what to say if I'd tried. It weren't Lewis's way to be open with his feelings. Happen he saw it as a weakness, like so many men do. 'They've gone soft,' he would have said, watching the neighbours herded out of their homes. 'It'd tek more than a gust of wind to blow me over.' He'd always had his courage. Courage is a gunshot cutting short the days you remember, a face-off with a storm in a house that might slip into the sea, take you with it.

I drift in and out of sleep. In the small hours, something comes crashing through the glass ceiling of the conservatory; a tree branch or a roof tile, I'm much too scared to check. Scared. It's a relief to admit it. I may be stubborn but I've never claimed to be fearless. I bolt the door closed and wedge the frame with blankets and cushions, poor defences against an incoming flood.

Sure as anything, morning comes. The day Lewis died, I sat up all night in the conservatory and watched the sun creep up the same way it always had. I stayed there until I could feel the warmth of it on my face. If I was of a religious leaning, I'd have took that as a sign of Lewis having reached the other side. But I knew it was just the universe doing what it did; no special meaning to it. This morning, the sky is grey and thick like newly shorn wool, no sun to speak of. I sit for a long time on the settee staring at the embers. 'I hope I've made you proud,' I say to Lewis, afloat in the North Sea, the pistol his father left him weighing heavy in his pocket.

I put on my wellies and walk through the conservatory. The roof tile slipped smoothly through the ceiling. Glass crunches wetly underfoot. I keep going. I can see the hydrangeas and the tarp that has somehow stayed in place. The ground feels like I could fall straight through it. Surviving a storm takes you closer to the rhythms of nature. You feel things others don't: seeds forcing through the earth beneath you, the change in the air before rain. The crumbling away of the soft-clay cliffs that have always held their own.

# The Weight of the Air

Celia shakes me awake. 'What is it?' I say. I grab for my phone on the nightstand. The screen shows a quarter past four.

'Shh, listen,' Celia says. Her fingers are still wrapped around my shoulder.

I hear many things in the darkness: the sway of the wind through the cypress trees that grow out of the shallows of the lake; the distant ticking of the kitchen clock whose batteries she insisted on replacing as soon as we got here yesterday evening. Nothing, though, to warrant the persistent grasping, the breath held in. 'Darlin', I can't hear a damn thing besides that clock—'

But there it is, and Celia tightens her grip for emphasis. A definite scuttling, claws against wood, coming from above. 'You believe me now?' she hisses, as I swing my legs out of the bed and touch my feet slowly to the hardwood floor. My old body aches at every joint.

In the deep of the night, I understand what the house must have felt like this past year. The hunting trophies – oh, how I hate those gruesome things – lurch from the walls, antlers bared. Beyond the windows in the sun room – Mama's pride and joy, and what pleasure it'd bring her to know that the bamboo lounge set is still fully intact! – the lake is still as a coin on the sidewalk. I follow the sound down the hallway and pause under the hatch leading up to the attic.

Celia is a shadow by the window when I walk back through to the sun room. I slump down into one of the chairs, dust scratching my eyes. 'Well, whatever it is is gon' be staying for a while.'

'Why? Where is it?' Celia says.

Again comes the skitting, or flitting; two years in Austin and there's nothing of these Delta backwaters left in me. 'In the attic, most likely.'

Celia sits down on the loveseat across from me. I hadn't wanted her to come, a truth that constricts me as I look at her folding her legs up underneath herself like a kitten by a fire. She's mighty bright for the early hour. I adore this about her in the city, but on this uneven land it grates. 'Well, you need to go up there anyway, don't you? Sure, the flood's not likely to reach quite so far but like I said in the car, we may as well—'

'If the flood's not going to reach it, why'd I need to clear it?'

She thinks about this for a moment. 'I suppose that's true. Besides, with Angie's room still full of her things there's plenty to—'

'Would you just drop it, Celia?' I say. The kitchen clock snaps from one second to the next. I wonder how long it kept going after I left. A guilty softness spreads through my stomach. 'Why don't we go back to bed, think about it some more in the morning.'

She looks at me then, a look that contains every moment of the year we've spent together. I know that's what it holds because I know my own mind can do the same thing, spiralling within seconds through every kindness or transgression enacted towards me. The cypress trees whisper by the window. 'You got it, Junie,' she says, and when she walks past, she rests her hand on my shoulder, palm springing away in a beat.

We wrestle against morning for an hour or two, rising as the sun reaches its rays across the water, twinkling over the duckweed. As I crack an egg on the skillet, Celia twists the dial of the old radio that sits on the kitchen table. *That's exactly right, Janice. In fact, the farmers we spoke to over in Warren County are preparing for the total decimation of their crops. Switching to the West Coast for a minute, though, an evil of a whole other kind has Southern California in its grip –*

'California! Oh Junie, ain't that where Angie is?'

*– to spread across the state. According to local reports, firefighters are struggling to keep the blaze under control. While no human lives have yet been lost, the effect on wildlife has been described as –*

'Turn it off, would you?' I say, scraping the egg onto a slice of bread. The butter boils on the surface of the skillet, a stray blob bursting off and onto my wrist. 'Shit.'

*– well, Janice, it remains unclear whether or not evacuation orders will be issued –*

'Turn it off, please, Celia.' The voices twist away as she turns the dial.

Celia sits down at the table, folds her arms one on top of the other. 'Do you think we have enough time?'

I put the plate of eggs down in front of her. 'The removal van is booked for Thursday. That gives us three days.'

It's hard to imagine the heat – which, at not even eight in the morning, is already burning up on our skin – will break for the type of apocalyptic rainfall predicted. We'd dropped everything when the reports first gained traction, clearing diaries and work schedules, loading flattened boxes into the back of the rented Range Rover. Celia had waved her hand at me when I'd asked if she was sure she could miss her client meetings so close to the end of the quarter; as for me, the Dean might as well have cheered when I told her I'd be absent from my lecturing duties for the week.

'You know,' Celia says, resting her knife and fork on the edge of the plate. 'If I was the good little believer my Mama and Daddy wanted me to be, I'd say these floods are an act of wrath.'

I picture the fields under water; miles of old plantation land, submerged.

Angie had chosen California for the distance. She had friends there, she'd said, people who'd help her find her way. I'd been grateful to have at least been afforded that scrap of information. 'Oh, she's hurtin',' Celia said soon after we met, when the wound of Angie's leaving was still open, stinging with the tenderness of falling in love. Well, who ain't? I sip my coffee, look out at the lake. We all have pain. But the pain in me is not the same pain that runs through my daughter, or Celia. It's not the same pain Mama lived with during those long months of dying. Even if it was that we all share a common wound, inflicted by a singular power, it would still be true that we weather the pain of it differently. Angie weathers hers five states away, as far from the source as she can get.

'Junie,' Celia whispers, beckoning me from my spot in the sun room. 'Tread lightly, honey.'

I put my cup of coffee down on the glass-top side table and follow her out onto the porch. The redwood planks are hot as coals on my bare soles. No further than ten feet away from us, a pair of deer are grazing on the overgrown grass at the edge of the tree line. I don't exactly share Celia's childlike wonder, but the way their graceful bodies bend towards the ground does something to my mood that I can't quite explain. They seem undisturbed by our presence, as though with its custodians gone, the house has been reclaimed, the bottomlands it was built on taken back. The heat from the wood is too much to bear, and the movement of me lifting one foot then the other eventually spooks the deer. I think about the man who cut these redwoods down, stripped them back and nailed them together. His malice haunts every inch of the house; no flood would be enough to wash him out.

Celia strokes a hand down my back. 'Let's get started.'

We start in the living room, Dolly's sweet little voice spinning out from the record player. We rifle through years-old editions of the *Clarksdale Press Register*, folded over on the obits. Mama always wondered how they'd write her up in the end. By lunch, we've gutted the drawers of the old walnut dresser, wrapped every last bit of antique china and collected curiosity. I can feel the pull of nostalgia; I recognise it in the familiar pattern of a pillow packed away, or the grain of a wooden photo frame that feels just as I remember. When we get to the kitchen, it's worse. I pull jars of pickles out from the back of the pantry, Mama's handwriting displaying dates that far precede her passing. I toss the jars straight into the trash, Celia eyeing me warily from the other side of the room. I think about when Mama was going: long, hot days like these ones, our waiting bodies sweating like the devil himself, Angie dabbing lavender onto her wrists at this very same table. We've been here two days and I still haven't opened the doors to either of their rooms.

In the living room, Dolly's begging that wily Jolene to show mercy. Celia lands a kiss on the back of my neck. 'Let's take a break.'

*

My dreams are all watery, pushing me up to the surface at some cursed hour of the night. I realise, as my brain adjusts to wakefulness, that I dreamed about Charlie. It was the flood, the one that came the day he left us; the crunch of his truck on the driveway, returning an hour later to help us load our lives into the back. In that slippery way of dreams, it's not the full sequence of events that I dreamed of, but snippets: the knowledge that the rain was on its way, the panic at knowing we were stranded. There's nothing quite as awkward as dreaming about your ex-husband while your lover snores gently beside you. I look over at the solid, real shape of Celia, turned onto her side, the wisps of hair against the wrinkled skin of her neck.

The floorboards creak where they always have, a sound as familiar to me as my own name. In the sun room, the noise of the lake grows louder: frogs croaking at the surface, that reliable breeze in the cypresses. I keep going down the hallway. I'm not scared; who'd be scared of just pushing the door to a bedroom open, walking in? 'We all have pain to face up to,' Celia would probably say. I turn the doorknob and wait to be sucked through a portal to the past.

The smell hits me first, a staleness that hangs in the air. I don't remember closing the door after Angie left but I must have. Her comforter sits in the centre of the bed, curled over like whipped cream. Some of the posters have unpeeled themselves from the walls, hanging sadly from one determined blob of tack. Her bulletin board is still leaning against the wall on the vanity. I don't look at it – I can't – but I marvel at the resilience of things, how gravity and tension continue to exist behind closed doors to hold everything in place. I can still see the shape of her, standing over the bed, throwing t-shirts and jeans into an overnight bag that has clothed her for a whole year.

I'm jogged out of my memories by a rustling, that same sound we heard last night. We had squirrels in the attic once; a whole gang of them, biting through the beams. Me and Mama begged him to spare them but his taste for blood had no limits. Six I remember him catching, every trap we owned called in for duty. He had one stuffed for me as a gift that Christmas. It's probably in one of the boxes up there, between fleece-lined flannel shirts and the letters he sent me from prison, unopened, one every month until he died.

'Holy Mother of God,' Celia says from the doorway, hand against her chest.

'I think it might be squirrels,' I say, though it could just as well be rats, or racoons.

What would you save from a fire or a flood or some other act of natural destruction? I never imagined I'd be asking myself that question for real. But what would you save if, truly, you wanted it all to disappear into ash or mulch? I deal with Angie's clothes, folding them quickly into a box, trying not to pay attention to the colours and fabrics. 'Oh,' Celia says, pulling Polaroids away from the bulletin board. 'Look at this one.' But I don't turn around, and eventually I hear the sound of the photo being added to the pile.

Celia had so many questions at the start. Our first date was embarrassingly public: a walk around campus after she'd given a lecture on future economics to a class that was either hungover or baked. When I said I had a grad school-aged daughter, she'd looked searchingly at the lines on my face, at the greys that sprung many years prior. I could have made it easy for her, but it wasn't – still ain't – an easy story to tell. Neither is the story of why Angie left, a question that again hangs between us as we pack away opposite corners of her – and once my – childhood room.

We spent another year with Charlie after that earlier flood. He moved us up to the mountains, where Angie learned to fish and dive headfirst into lakes. She belonged there more than anywhere else, but California is the place she chose. Moving a thirteen-year-old back to the Delta and into her grandmother's house was the kind of crime that'd see you locked away for a lifetime. Everything sucked: school sucked, the biting flies sucked, the damp air and the swamp smell of the forest sucked. Then later, resentment turned into something far more dangerous to a hungry mind: curiosity. *Who are our ancestors? How did they get here? Why don't you or Gramma ever talk about Grampa? Why did he go to jail?*

After lunch, we go for a walk through the forest. Woodpeckers twang against the cottonwoods, prompting Celia to stop every two minutes and point towards the canopy. If it didn't feel like the sky was pushing down on me I might be able to bask in the sweetness with which she moves through this difficult place, seeing only the remarkable. But I remember these woods only as a place of escape, the burn of his hand still hot against my cheek. 'Watch out for snakes,' I say, and we don't go much further after that before turning back.

The next room we deal with is Mama's. Oh, it's full of ghosts: Angie, lifting her grandmother's arm to run a damp cloth down the length of her skin; Mama, on that last night, clutching my wrist, *I shoulda done more to stop him, Junie.* I jostle them out of the way as I dismantle the matching side lamps, pull the hat boxes down from the top of the closet. On the windowsill, a vase holds the rotten, wilted remains of handpicked prairie flowers. By the time we are done, the sun has sunk low in the sky and the cicadas are chirping loudly. After dinner, we take tumblers of Jim Beam out onto the porch. The alcohol smooths out my edges, and the words slide easily out of my mouth. 'I blamed Angie,' I say, batting a cloud of gnats away. 'She wanted to know about everything, towards the end. Mama didn't have no strength left in her to take all her questions.'

Celia is quiet. She doesn't even look in my direction, just twirls her glass, the liquid sloshing silently inside it. Eventually, she lets out a long sigh. 'And do you still?'

'Blame Angie?' I push my sunglasses onto my forehead and wipe a finger across my eyes. 'No. But I wish she'd understood. I don't ever want to tell her those things. I don't ever want to tell anyone those things. She pushed and she pushed and when I snapped it was bad. Yeah, it was bad.'

'And then she left?'

'And then she left.'

There's something about the weight of the air that feels like the heat is about to break. I want to roll the cool glass across my throat but I don't. The string lights Celia wrapped along the edge of the porch reflect on the top of the lake, flickering with the movement of the water like flames.

In the attic, there's an old photo album with a cracked leather case. I can feel the torn fabric just thinking about it. In the album, there's a picture of my father as a boy, holding a dogfish out to the camera, flashing a toothy kid's smile. The date scrawled on the back in my grandmother's handwriting reads 1936. The Delta, and the state, had gone through hard times and had yet more hard times up ahead. But before all of that there was, at one point long ago, peace. A perfect, harmonious peace; a child who hadn't yet learned the power that violence can yield. I wrote him a letter once. I was twenty one, and full of hurt, and wanted, or thought I wanted, to understand why. *He's got that same hate his father got, and his father before him*, Mama said. He was dead to her by then. I folded the letter away between the pages of the Bible he'd left me. It was easier that way, to act like he was dead; like he'd never been part of our lives, part of me.

In the end, it's laughably easy to go up there: just a series of actions one after the other that result in me crouching under the eaves, chinks of morning light piercing through. Behind tools and fishing equipment, three cardboard boxes are all that's left of him. I know, somewhere inside them, there's the Bible and the letters, the leather-bound album, the damn stuffed squirrel. These aren't things I want to lay my eyes on ever again, but I woke up this morning with a clarity I haven't felt in years; an instinct to preserve the worst of my personal history, if not for myself then for someone else.

From the bottom of the ladder, Celia's voice calls up. 'Oh, honey. You did it.'

I rest a hand on one of the boxes, the cardboard flap spongy with mildew, anticipating rain. There's an emptiness inside me that this house feeds off, and suddenly I am euphoric to be leaving today. A cautious rustling is coming from somewhere. 'Y'all won this time,' I whisper.

Later, while the movers pack every last bit of furniture into their lorry, Celia and I stand on the porch and look out at the clouds gathering over the lake. Celia suggests we go through each room to say goodbye. 'There's no way of telling when you might next be here,' she says.

Practical matters push at my thoughts: repairs that need doing, the future nightmare of selling an old house grown out of a flood-plain. As the movers close up the back of the truck, I glimpse the bamboo limbs of the lounge set that will soon be starting a new life in a storage unit in Austin. 'I just want to get on the road,' I say, and Celia's face scrunches up, knotted with a yearning to tell me I'm making a big mistake. But, bless her heart, she stays quiet, squeezes my hand tight in hers instead.

Raindrops begin to appear on the windscreen just as we cross state lines. In the passenger seat, Celia drifts in and out of sleep, her head tilting forward only to be jerked back upright. I turn on the radio for the afternoon news. *Evacuation orders have been issued to some 15,000 residents in Southern California as wildfires continue to rip through the state.* My heart aches for Angie, my late baby, born long after I'd given up hope. I turn off the highway and pull into a dirt path that runs along an unploughed field. From the boot, I hear the smooth shift of boxes, my father's things hidden inside.

Celia stirs. 'What's going on?'

I take out my phone and bring up the number; oh, the bargaining I'd had to do to squeeze it out of one of her friends. 'I – I have to do this,' I say, my voice bubbling with tears.

*For emergencies only*, I'd promised, and I'd kept my word a whole year. A year is a long time; long enough for a phone to slip out of your hand and shatter on the sidewalk. Long enough for a mother to start forgetting the sound of her daughter's laugh. I want to tell her about the boxes in the back; to commit, finally, to letting her ask, even if I can't find the answers right away. I want to say, Hey, why don't we take a trip up to the mountains, you always loved it there. I want to hear she's OK, watching the fires on a screen someplace safe. I want to hit call, I really do.

I open the car door and step out. Miles of soybean fields stretch as far as the eye can see; they brace themselves for a downpour, rain with the might of a thousand flames. Let's meet in the middle, I'll tell her, somewhere dry and cool. I turn my face up to the clouds, up to the rain that is coming quicker now from that same sky we're all trying to live under.

# Monsters

Our breath hangs in the frosty mid-March air as we leave the pond. Our towel-dried hair isn't dry enough; I'll catch a well-meaning remark about that at the school gates, no doubt. Bessie is dragging her feet, skipping the cracks in the pavement. I don't know what she thinks might happen if she steps on them. I don't want to ask. She swings her book bag out in front of her, the shiny fabric swishing against her trousers. 'Did you see Scally today?' she says.

Ahead of us, cars and buses move through an amber light. 'Who?'

'Scally.'

'Details, please. Who's Scally? And knock it off with the cracks.'

Bessie lets go of my hand and stops walking. The front of her school jumper is damp from where her hair has soaked the fabric. 'She lives in the pond. I thought you would have seen her by now.'

'We're running late, come on,' I say, and we reach the crossing which is again somehow on a green light, traffic flooding through. 'What's Scally, then, a fish or something?'

'No,' Bessie scoffs. 'She's so much more than a fish.'

'More than a fish? OK, an eel? A bird? Do I get a prize if I guess correctly?'

'Well, she's kind of hard to describe. She has these horns . . .'

'Horns? What you on about?'

'Let me finish! She has horns, and scales, and a huge tail,' she says, pausing in thought. 'Oh, and fins, like a shark's? She has those all down her spine.'

When you lower yourself into the pond this time of year, for a second, it feels like your blood has frozen in your veins. I get that feeling now, by the crossing that has finally given us permission to walk.

Bessie was born into water. I think of her birth when I plunge my body into the pond, breathe in and out through the stabbing cold. Last month, when she turned eight, she did her competency test, so she could swim with me in the mornings. She loves how the reeds at the edge of the water sound when the wind riffles through them. 'Like they're whispering,' she says to me. 'Telling each other secrets.' She's not squeamish about the muddy film that sticks itself to our arms or the green smell of the water. 'My little mermaid,' Blake used to call her. He'd know what to do about Scally.

Scally, I've come to learn, lives in a cave at the bottom of the pond. She watches our breakfast-full bellies bobbing at the surface. She's not a monster – very important – and now she needs our help. 'If we don't save the planet then the pond will die and Scally won't have anywhere to go,' Bessie tells me the next day as she folds her Aertex shirt in our kit bag, spreading a thumb over the thick threads of the school emblem.

'Can't she live in the sea? There's plenty of space there,' I say, thinking of waves crashing far beyond the pier.

On the deck by the side of the pond, I bend to scrape Bessie's curls into a bun. We're early today, but not as early as Meredith, who is cutting through the water like scissors through a length of silk. The frown on Bessie's face tells me I've got it wrong again. 'Too salty. Her scales would fall off.'

I change tack. 'How old is Scally?'

Bessie heads towards the edge of the deck. She knows not to jump in the water until I'm in there first. 'Old. Older than time itself.'

I ease myself down the ladder. 'Wouldn't that make her older than the pond?'

'OK, fine, she's as old as the pond,' Bessie says, sitting down and dangling her legs off the side. 'She was born when the pond was created.'

The water feels like a pane of glass shattering. 'So she has a mummy, like me?'

'The pond is her mummy,' Bessie says, plopping down into the pond with a squeal.

We keep ourselves afloat, swimming in close circles while we acclimatise to the biting chill. Bessie dips her head under the water, and for once, I don't worry she might not come back up. Another mother is looking out for her now, after all.

In Brighton, we used to go to the sea every morning. Sometimes we'd just roll up our trousers and walk into the shallows; other times we'd wearily yank on our wetsuits and bob about in the waves, eyes stinging with the splash of saltwater. It was here that Bessie formed an affinity with cold bodies of water. Blake would hold her ankles and I'd hold her elbows and we'd watch her, learning to float. Within weeks, she could kick her feet out behind her and paddle from one of us to the other. Sometimes, we'd buy a bag full of doughnuts to treat her on the way home, Blake holding a finger to his sugary lips. 'Don't tell your teachers.'

The water that comes out of the hot tap is as cold as that morning sea. It's the third time in as many months that the boiler has broken; since we've been here, we've had no faith in warm showers. In the winding stairwells and walkways of the estate, neighbours exchange tips for dealing with the housing association for a chance to pinch Bessie's cheeks or fuss over the burst of her curls. I learn about other gripes: a community garden riddled with bindweed, rumours of private investment and development plans. Our neighbours mellow to our presence; we're invited for tea, called upon to borrow emergency onions. But the flat wants us out; it says so by way of the broken boiler, and the golden moths that we find in the folds of our clothes and burrowing in the corners of the carpeted rooms.

'It's so lovely that Bessie and Agnes are in the same class,' Meredith says next time we go to the pond. We're sipping steaming coffee on the deck, our bare feet leaving puddles beneath us. Bessie is cross-legged on the floor, reading a book about birds that live in marshes, thriving by the water. Agnes doesn't come to the morning swims because her nanny, Wilhelmina, is a 'lifesaver', getting her ready and off to Saint Gregory's, the state school our children both go to. By all accounts, she's a wonderful kid; although, according to Bessie, she 'smells like farts'.

Meredith has been swimming at the pond for six years. 'We've seen lots of newcomers pass through. They're very enthusiastic for a month or so, then, like clockwork, they drop away, never to be seen again.'

It feels like a warning, an unspoken code of conduct to honour the pond and its dependents. I think about the waves lapping at the shore on the coast. Had the sea seen our leaving as a betrayal?

'But you don't seem like that,' Meredith adds, her green eyes sparkling above the rim of her cup.

I walk home slowly from dropping Bessie at school, going down side streets that take me past boutique cafes with metal tables folded out on the pavement. Women carry bouquets of multicoloured tulips wrapped in brown paper or loaves of artisanal bread. I'm a lady of leisure like them, but my days are dictated by job centre appointments and long applications and instant coffees left unattended on the kitchen counter. 'You'll find something soon,' Meredith had said. 'Maybe I can ask Wilhelmina if she knows of any nanny jobs going?'

At home, I make an omelette for lunch, taking quick bites while I bookmark admin and office management roles with salaries that barely stretch to cover a month's costs. Guilt swipes at me: it was Blake who gave us the money for a summer pass at the pond. 'Don't let Bessie forget how to swim,' he'd said, though I know this gift was meant just as much for me. In return, I think of him whenever I'm in the water, slippery memories of our time together tracing my laps back and forth. He'd be sailing out to the oil field soon, banners and megaphone at the ready. After that, there'd be another evil force to contend with. Sometimes I feel foolish for thinking what we have now is any more stable than what staying with him might have been like.

\*

Something's wrong with Meredith the next time I see her. She knows I'm in the pond; it's just us two, as usual. But where she normally gives me a glance or a wave, today she keeps her focus on the heavy breadth of water ahead. Gradually, others trickle in: Lucie, whose husband's cancer is advancing; Gosia, back now her skin has healed, the dark lines of an indecipherable tattoo needling their way down her shoulder. They each receive a nod, that friendly warmth I've come to look for in Meredith given easily.

She catches up with me on the deck as I'm stirring milk into a cup of tea.

'So, listen,' she says, peeling her swimming cap off. 'Can I speak to you about something quickly?'

My skin prickles. 'Yeah, sure.'

Meredith looks genuinely pained. A flush of cold floods me as it occurs to me that she might be about to cry. 'Agnes was a little upset yesterday after school, because of something Bessie told her.'

Instinctively, I search for Bessie's presence by my side, only to remember that she's with Val next door this morning. 'Oh, OK.'

'Now I know children tend to have very creative imaginations, especially at this age. So I'm sure Bessie didn't mean anything by it . . .'

'It's OK, Meredith, just tell me what she said.'

That same expression settles on her face, and I think of those caricatures artists draw on Parisian streets. 'Well, she told Agnes that there's a sea creature of some sort, at the bottom of the pond. And that humans are destroying her home.'

'Not a sea creature,' I say before thinking. 'She doesn't tolerate saltwater.'

Meredith laughs thinly. A speck of leaf has stuck itself to her cheek. 'Did you know about this?'

'It's harmless,' I say, closing my hand around the side of the mug.

'Not when it results in my child coming home in tears,' she says, turning away from me to where her towel has blown.

A sudden cool breeze chills me. Meredith has been the most accepting of the regular swimmers. We live on different planets, but under the warmth of her sun I forget about the lightyears of difference between us. I watch her scrub her skin dry, droplets of water running down the backs of her thighs.

As I'm heading back inside with my cup, she puts a damp hand on my arm. 'I know things are very . . . intense right now. The climate is a very hot topic, for want of a better word. But perhaps you might think about shielding Bessie from some of the scarier news? Clearly it's making an impression and it's hard to see how these kinds of fantasies can be helpful.'

I force a smile. 'I'll think about that. Thanks. And sorry.'

'That's OK,' she says, wafting her hand through the air. 'Oh, I meant to ask. Did you find any work yet?'

'Still looking,' I say, turning away from her pitying eyes, towards the shapes of the other women moving through the water.

We're treading water in the middle of the pond when raindrops start to pock its surface. Earlier that morning, we'd drunk cartons of apple juice on the walkway outside the front door, marvelling at the spectral mist that drifted over the rooftops below us. It'd been like that for a week, always clearing into hazy spring sunshine. Through the open door, I could hear the news reporting from the far reaches of the North Sea, on the rig they'd built off the Shetland coast. Blake had been willing to give up his life to oppose it. Now, our lives revolve around different bodies of water, but still I feel moored to the pier that had once been the backdrop to our shared swims.

Where the willows brush the water, Meredith skims across the pond like a pebble. Heather, the lifeguard, is calling us in from the deck. 'Come on, Bessie, time to swim back,' I say. As we glide towards the sound of Heather's voice, the raindrops grow in number and weight, falling quick and fat on our shoulders. I think about our kit bag, left open on the deck, Bessie's uniform exposed to the elements. I remember being warned not to swim during or after rainfall; at the time, I wrote it off as superstition, but as fear spreads through my limbs I start to understand.

'Scally likes the mist,' Bessie had said, drawing golden liquid up through her straw. 'She likes the way it feels on her scales.' Scally isn't Bessie's first imaginary friend. There've been others: a twin sister, Jessie, had lived with us for several months during the Year of Isolation; then, after the move to Brighton, a feathered mouse called Pip Squeak had helped her settle in. In the newspapers, fancy writers with doctorates were always coining new psychological conditions for the kids born into lockdowns and pandemics and climate disasters, but all I knew was that my daughter seemed to have found a creative way to deal with the horrors of the world around her. I envied her that, sometimes.

Above us, the sky has turned suddenly dark. The space between the water and the heavy black clouds feels tight, even more so when the first growl of thunder erupts. I can barely hear Heather's voice now over the lashing rain, so I don't hear straight away that Meredith is calling my name, screaming it, waving her hand against the swaying branches of the willows. I angle my body towards her and notice that Bessie's no longer behind me; she's nowhere.

I cut through the thick swell of the water, barely breathing, Meredith's waving arms blending into the reeds. Somewhere in the motion of my arms, in the pushing of my feet against the stronghold of the pond, I realise just how happy I'd be to die this very moment if it meant that Bessie made it back to the deck in one piece. It's always felt like such a hypothetical thing, that commitment of parents to lay down their lives for their children. But I know now that I'd drown in a heartbeat so that she might never see the underside of the pond, that unknowable world down there.

In the watery distance, I see Bessie's face at the surface, blurred through tears and snot and rain.

We hoist ourselves onto the deck and lie there, splayed, newborns pulled from one world into another. Heather bundles us into towels and pushes us towards the changing room, but Bessie breaks away, flings her towel to the ground.

'What did I tell you, Bessie?' I say. 'Never swim out of my sight. Why didn't you listen?'

'You don't care about Scally,' Bessie shouts, tears streaming down her cheeks. 'You don't care that rain makes the pond poisonous and that she might die in there!'

'Ladies, get inside, now,' Heather says, another crash of thunder rolling from the clouds.

'Of course I care, but I care about you more. You scared the shit out of me just now!'

Meredith, the only one of us who'd heeded Heather's instruction to take shelter inside, comes back out and points a wet finger at me. 'You need to stop encouraging this sea monster nonsense, it's putting your child's life in danger.'

'Meredith, please,' I say, my voice trembling.

'No, I'm sorry, but I won't stay silent on this!' Meredith says. 'You're indulging in a fantasy that nearly caused your daughter to drown!'

'Ladies, that's enough!' Heather says, furious; broad arms reaching out for us again.

'She's not a monster. You're the monsters!' Bessie says, stamping a bare foot against the deck. It's then that the sky splits open, a flash of lightning forking down onto the surface of the pond, forcing us all into terrified silence.

It's no small mercy that the boiler is working today, because we stand in the shower for a very long time, hot water raining down onto our shivering bodies. I call the school and blame Bessie's absence on a dodgy tummy, then stir cocoa powder into milk on the cooker. The rain carries on outside, but up here we feel fortified against it, safe behind a barrier of concrete and brick. We spend most of the day on the sofa, duvets pulled in from our bedrooms, dozing off between animated films that play at a low volume on the TV. When I jolt awake, I think about the white bolt of lightning. It had come from somewhere so far out of our reach, stretched from one dimension to another.

Once Bessie's in bed, I crawl back under my duvet and switch to the news channel. The footage circles above the new rig, its metal frame braced against ferocious waves. I'd said I wouldn't call, and he'd agreed; it'd be easier to sever ties that way, keep things clean. But when I bring up Blake's number and press call, he picks up after one ring. 'Hey you,' he says, voice gleaming.

The lingering cold melts away from my bones. 'Hey,' I say.

We're silent for several moments. It's a silence thick with something like fate, a mutual understanding that this call would happen sooner or later. 'Where are you?' I say, quiet.

'I'd show you, but the camera won't do it justice. Plus, I don't think the connection here's strong enough for video.'

'You made it to Shetland, then, I take it?'

'We're at this farm,' Blake says. He sounds alive with hope. 'The family's letting us stay, really decent people.'

On the coffee table in front of me are four empty mugs – two each – lined with the grainy remains of hot chocolate. 'You must be in your element. You love a good farm.'

'They've got these sheep, proper characters they are. You'd love it here, Button.'

It's the nickname he gave me in the weeks after we met. It's always struck me how something as mundane as my inability to ever button up my clothes straight could become so laden with meaning and affection; so tender in the wake of a break-up neither of us had really wanted. I chew the inside of my cheek. I can feel the scraping of tears on the roof of my mouth.

Blake breaks the silence. 'I, uh, I'm looking out the window right now, right, and there's just stars, as far as the eye can see. No smog, no smoke. Just stars.'

I stand up and walk over to the window. Filtered through the double-glazing, the sky is muddy and inky, an upside-down pond. Its inverted surface glows with streetlights and headlights and the warmth of our homes; our living room lamps and naked bulbs, left on in error, swinging from bathroom ceilings. All throwing light into the world, lonely beacons looking for each other in the dark.

'How's my little mermaid?' Blake says, clearing his throat.

I've longed for the sounds of his body: the particular way he sighs after yawning and whistles when he's trying to remember where something is. 'She misses you.'

'Oh, I miss her too, to the moon and back.'

Tears ripple through my voice. 'Do you miss me too?'

He doesn't speak straight away, but when he does, he says, 'To the moon and back, Button. To the moon and back.'

Scally has learned to adapt to storms. She was scared of the thunder at first, the way it boomed above the pond's fragile surface. And the lightning, crackling like fire, cutting through clouds and sometimes even shattering the water like a spear thrown through thin ice. That was the scariest of all. Heavy rainfall could flood nearby sewers; it helped bad bacteria thrive, things that could get into our stomachs, ears and eyes, make us sick. Make Scally sick, too.

'She can burrow now,' Bessie tells me, as we walk the winding path to the pond. 'When the storm comes back she's going to dig herself down and hide until it's safe to come out.'

It's been a month since we've been here, a month since the storm. A month of packing our things up, again, spinning vague excuses with neighbours and teachers to explain our imminent departure. 'Do the other kids go to school?' Bessie had asked when I told her.

'Not exactly,' I'd replied. 'But they still learn. They learn from trees, birds, insects, rocks, people . . . nature's lessons.'

It's early, barely dawn. The gate is padlocked shut, a lick of melting frost along its iron railing. The adrenaline that's been building in my chest gains speed, and I sweep Bessie up onto the railing, gripping her waist. 'OK, now jump down, carefully.' Her feet hit the dirt path with a muted thud.

'Your turn now, Mum,' Bessie says, exhilarated, a curl of hair whipping across her chin.

Tomorrow, we'll be heading down to Brighton in a borrowed van, where friends of Blake's will meet us, help us offload our things into his house. There'll be just enough time to dip our toes in the sea before the journey north begins; another body of water to say goodbye to, grit flecking our ankles in the shallows.

I grab hold of the railing and heave myself, one foot then the other, above it. This is the first of many crimes I'll commit; the first of countless fences I'll breach. Our future is full of acts of trespass; we'll reconfigure what's right and what's wrong, write new rules for ourselves and each other. Bessie reaches out for my hands and I give them to her, bend my knees when I land, like I've always been taught to.

Mist clings to the pond and the bare-branched trees and shrubs lining its edges. Soon, they'll burst into green, and the meadows will follow. We've never seen the pond over summer but we can imagine its beauty. We can picture ourselves there, heat on our skin, our changing bodies fed and held by the temperate water. On the deck, Bessie nestles herself against my side. 'Maybe Scally will burrow all the way up to Scotland, and find a pond there instead.'

'Maybe she will,' I say, pulling her closer. 'She'd be in very good company there.'

From the gate, we hear the sound of metal clanging, a chain snaking loose. 'Come on,' I say, and we creep behind the building, readying ourselves to bolt over another fence, into the uncharted land beyond.

# The Creek House

*Younglings found in litter, oddly kinos.* I remember that clue because I wrote it the day after Bertie brought the kittens to the creek house. First one I came up with that could actually be solved. Miss Winters chalked it up on the blackboard after class and scratched her hair loose with a pencil, trying to crack it. I ran all the way home but still missed supper, got a licking like no other from my mother.

Next morning I heard small stones landing on my window. I knew exactly where the stairs creaked loudest, was out and on my bicycle in less than a heartbeat. Bertie had found the creek house the previous spring. It was made up of three brick walls with a fourth caved in, half a roof letting in every weather. We'd gone to great lengths to keep it a secret, and had managed just fine, until the Myers boys found it, did what they did. I wrote a lot of clues after that.

Bertie had lifted a bottle of milk from her brother's dinner pail. There'd be hell to pay later but at least we had something to give them. She'd packed the kittens in a wicker basket her mother used to store linens. The weave's loose enough to let air in, she'd said. I wondered where she'd hidden the linens. The basket shook with movement and meowing but inside two were dead. Runts, Bertie said. *Dull work off to a bad start.* We buried them in the soft ground, too close to the brook, rinsed our hands off in the water.

People ask me: what makes the perfect clue? They think to be able to write good cryptic clues you need to complicate, confuse. But a good clue is simply an honest one. And, honestly, they're simple. Once you master the method, you're golden. I've always found clues much easier to understand than people. Well-written clues don't always say what they mean but should always mean what they say. People, on the other hand, rarely say what they want to or mean what they say when they do. Riddle me that.

Now, I don't want you thinking ill of Bertie. She had her reasons for what she did next. Her father had dumped those cats in a wooden crate and left them at the bottom of the lane for the foxes. He was not an easy man to stand up to, even if she had boxed them up under the cover of night. But the milk turned, untouched. We didn't have the money for more and had both endured a clap around the ear for taking her brother's. We'd pour sour drops onto our fingers but the little critters could barely open their mouths to try suckling. As a last resort, I pocketed a half-empty bottle of my mother's Jim Beam. I'd seen the wonders it could work on her, thought it might soothe them. But Bertie shook her head when I offered a capful to the kittens. We took a swig each, instead. I think that's what gave her the courage to take the basket out to the creek and tip it open over the running stream.

I've seen a lot of bad things in my life, but nothing quite as rotten as that. The sun was liquid gold in the water, the air had that anything-is-possible, start-of-summer smell to it. The kittens had no chance. They just bobbed along on the surface, so slowly I wanted to get down on all fours in the silt and push them under and away. I think maybe I did, muddied the knees of the powder-blue capris my Aunt Jacqui had sent in the post. Paid the price for that at home, no doubt.

Bertie lost a bit of herself after that. She never said so, but I knew she was sorry. When the Myers boys followed our bicycle tracks out to the creek house one late afternoon, she didn't even try to fight back. Perhaps that was a worse thing to see than the kittens drowning in the stream. She pulled one shoe off then the other, let her shorts crumple in the corner, embroidered shirt to follow. Naked as the day she was born, she gave me a look as though this was her penance. I still don't quite know why they spared me. Could be they knew the cruelty in making us choose.

Once they were gone, I picked up Bertie's clothes and followed her out to the stream. I'd never seen anyone naked, not even my own mother. She had a lot more hair than I had. Darker, too. She walked straight into the creek, brought a cupped hand of water to the trickle of blood on her thigh. It didn't feel right just watching, so I stripped out of my clothes and stepped in. I remember it being shockingly cold, but the water in that section was only ankle deep and you could see right through to the glossy stones at the bottom. God strike me down but it felt like a kind of baptism. Every sin forgiven, washed clean by the stream.

She was gone from class a week before I plucked up the guts to ask after her. I left early one morning and found her father in his garage, arms slick with engine oil. The boarding school they'd sent her to was three counties away. She'd be home at Christmas, he said, and I tried to keep count of the days, watching the leaves turn and fall from the trees. True enough, though, I caught sight of her at Midnight Mass, hair set all fancy, crisp cotton collar on her velveteen dress. We had so much to say to each other and yet we said nothing at all. She was a clue I couldn't crack, not for want of trying; though as the years went by she dimmed in my memory, as I expect I did in hers.

The summer I graduated high school, I found work as a setter at the *New York Times* and lodgings with my Aunt Jacqui in Greenwich Village. There weren't many female setters working at that time but, hidden behind a pseudonym, no one was the wiser. My clue-setting smarts kept my head above water but in every other respect I was drowning. I'd gone from being a gawmy child cycling down dirt paths to get to wherever she needed to go, to a young woman with an unfamiliar city at her feet. I felt ashamed of how small my world had once been. It's not something I'm proud of but I did try to hide what I'd come from. I told all these tall tales about my father being an Arctic explorer whose remains were fossilised under metres of snow, and how my mother had died young, broken-hearted. It was during those years in New York that I discovered men and what I was willing to do for a moment of a man's attention. I gave myself over gladly, but they never stuck around for long. Could be that a part of me felt like it was a debt I owed. Aunt Jacqui had to call in favours from her physician friends a number of times to help me out of sticky situations.

The first postcard arrived the Christmas of '73. *Greetings From London*, it said across the front in big, black letters, Buckingham Palace topped with snow. Just as I'd found my metropolis, Bertie had also found hers. And in all of it, she'd thought of me, the girl she used to kick about the creek house with, when the world was no bigger than the land we could cover by bike. 'My mother sends me clippings of your crosswords from the paper,' she wrote. 'Only a masochist would attempt to complete such a thing.' That made me laugh. I'd never thought of cryptics as an act of self-loathing. I'd always found people much harder to endure.

We exchanged postcards all the time after that, each one like a clue that unlocked a little window into our lives. We had things to tell each other again. I followed her to Dublin, Paris, Madrid. In Scotland, she eloped with a dentist named Jerry she'd met on a skiing holiday in the Italian Alps. I buried my mother and travelled the West Coast on a shoestring. We shared every one of our losses and joys on those little pieces of card. We became different people, worn hard and soft by the weather of life.

Fifty years' worth of postcards is quite a collection. Some might say it's an eccentric way to stay in touch with your oldest friend. I've thought about calling, believe me, thought about hopping on a plane. I understand Bertie's need for distance. Could be I'm better at reading people than I thought I was. I wonder what her voice might sound like now: bastardised New England drawl. She works her way into clues sometimes, turning up in anagrams or wordplay. A good clue is one that stays with you, whether you remember it with fondness or pain, or both.

I think of the creek house often, with its stoved-up walls and rotted roof, brook full of squaretails come to spawn in the fall. I remember us as girls, hair wild, the soles of our feet hard and muddy. It was a broken, forgotten place but life ran through it, and it was more sacred to us in those days than any church or home. I've often thought of returning. Imagine us standing with our feet in the stream, trousers rolled up over wrinkled skin and knobbly knees. The water flows strong and quick around us, and I hold Bertie's hand and make a promise to never let go. No matter where the current takes us.

# Bound For Somewhere Else

Lily was not sure how, but somehow, she knew what happened at breakfast was her doing. She'd smelled the fried sweetness of the coconut bakes before she'd seen them, nestled softly together in the bread basket where there should have been miniature baguettes, or brioche buns. The bakes at least were easy enough to ignore, but the plates of fleshy saltfish, fragrant with chopped peppers, spring onions and thyme, were decisively not.

The other attendees feigned polite curiosity. They'd been expecting the usual continental fare: stale croissants, strips of stringy bacon tonged from the hotplate. They held their conference lanyards flat against their chests and bent to inspect the strange food. Next to her, a man with butter-blond hair – everything pale, even the wispy hint of his eyebrows – took a deep breath in. He seemed to be enjoying the confusion. 'Looks like some of them will go hungry this morning.' By the buffet table, a woman in a tight, black skirt appeared distressed as she tried to catch the eye of a member of staff. A wave of shame hit Lily then, so hard she felt the frothy wash of it spread over the pointed toes of her patent-leather heels.

Given that she'd come to the conference as a last-minute stand-in, it was especially frustrating to think she might not be able to leave. Light-hearted commentary among the attendees about the relentless snowfall had taken on a more serious tone, and the organisers had been forced to address the matter before the day's events began. They'd be monitoring the weather, they said, but felt sure that it was nothing to worry about. Tacked onto the end of that announcement was an apology about the breakfast buffet. 'We're consulting with our food contractors to ensure there are no further mix-ups.'

She'd laughed along nervously with the others, because not doing so meant thinking about what had actually happened, which was, however implausible, that she had conjured the saltfish and the bakes from the recesses of childhood memory. In the static snowstorm blowing horizontally outside the expansive glass windows of the hotel, she had seen low clouds slung across rolling hills. She anchored herself in the dim light of the auditorium: folding chairs, projector, fire exit. Snow was expected here for April, but not in this quantity. Keynote speaker, slide deck, hashtag. She shifted in her seat. Under her crisp white shirt, her limbs were wreathed in mist.

She'd been there just once, as a child, to this place she was half from. To be half from somewhere felt to Lily like a strange quantification of something that couldn't easily be quantified. But it was, always had been, the way she described herself to others when prompted; that persistent question that often revealed itself on the tongues of strangers, eager to categorise. She could feel their curiosity as she ate her lunch – smoked salmon on rye bread, side salad dressed with too much lemon – in the cafeteria. She was sure, amidst the clang of cutlery and stilted corporate conversation, she could hear the brush of sticks against steelpan.

The blond man put his plate down at the seat next to hers and gestured towards the stool. 'May I join you?'

She smiled through a mouthful of bread. 'Of course.'

Outside, the skeletal pines were barely visible behind the filter of constant white. 'I heard the conference next week has been cancelled.'

She straightened her back. 'That doesn't surprise me.'

'At least we'll be able to eat their food,' he said, spearing a boiled potato.

A thought came to her then; the vision of a banquet of ripened fruit. 'I'm sure it won't come to that.'

'You seem so sure we won't be permanently snowed in here,' he said, the warmth of a smile in his voice. 'Shame, I was looking forward to having you as a neighbour.'

Lily folded her napkin neatly over her plate, felt the woven weight of it plush on her fingertips. It was, she knew, absurd to think there might be a chance they'd be stuck here for any meaningful period of time, but it was a thought she felt strangely at peace with. She'd always been good at putting her life into boxes. No place had been home for longer than two years before it was time to pack up again, move on. Her aerial roots were well fed on the flora and fauna of the cities and countries she passed through: cycling to the harbour in Christianshavn; marvelling at the *sakura* in Shinjuku. But here, she had landed what most people would view as a serious job with serious prospects. She'd surprised herself by finding the same fulfilment in leading meetings and helping clients that she'd once looked for in unfamiliar places.

In the window, the strip lights reflected a translucent glow. Time had lost its shape in the snow; it could, Lily thought, just as easily have been the early hours of the morning as midday. Later, in the sterile darkness of her hotel room, the shapelessness loomed. She drew back the heavy curtain and watched the blizzard continue its assignment. There were eighty other people attending the conference; eighty people who might, at that very moment, also have been touching their noses to the glass, seeking intimacy with the elements. Perhaps, Lily thought, they'd never seen anything like this before either. Perhaps they were as compelled by the unfamiliar as she was, drawn ever closer to it in the middle of the night.

This was a feeling Lily knew well. She tasted it in the phantom heat of a scotch bonnet pepper on her tongue, or in the bruised scent of a mango freshly picked from her cousin's garden. It pulled at her like sand sifting out from beneath her feet in the shallows. Its persistence struck her as punishment. She resented the chasm that had grown where there should have been connection, the fact that she only remembered in emblematic snippets. In all her wandering, she'd revisited only in memory. To be half from somewhere sometimes felt like being from nowhere at all.

In the coolness of the room, her skin sang with the evening heat of the panyard where, many years ago, she'd danced at the knee of her father.

Lily had not left the hotel for three days. The smokers were the only ones who saw their cause worthy enough of braving it; they'd come back in snowflaked and smiling, but subdued, as though some awful truth had been bared in the whiteout they couldn't put into words. It was in their bones now, she thought; now they would know how it felt.

Whiteout: that was the technical term for what they observed from the foyer on their mid-morning coffee break. Any discernible outlines – parked cars, distant pylons – had been swallowed by a powder cloud, snow worked up into a cyclone frenzy to hang, suspended, in the air. Warmth spilled from teak-panelled walls and low, soft jazz played from invisible speakers. Lily drank the bitter coffee and drifted between conversations of varying catastrophic proportions. In one, a woman fidgeted with her lanyard while she talked about the time she'd been confined to a hotel during an earthquake in Tokyo. 'I knew it was the safest place I could be,' she said. 'But it still felt like a cage.'

Lily pulled at her own lanyard. It felt absurd that the conference was still going, that they were all still wearing lanyards, but the thought of shedding the last pretences of normality churned in the pit of her stomach. In the milky morning light, she'd dabbed foundation onto her skin, drawn her eyes into sharp points, and strung her lanyard around her neck; dutifully, the plastic slip projected her name like a beacon. The borders of their corporate dimension blurred with the snowstorm: sales forecasts, PowerPoints, whiteout, blizzard, I'll hand you over to the CEO of You Might Never Leave This Hotel. By the window, a man's flight had been cancelled, news he announced to the room in a flurry of expletives. She could feel it prickling at the back of her neck, civility crumbling.

In her pocket, her phone felt stone-heavy. Home was somewhere she called on birthdays or when she'd had too much to drink and wanted to hear her mother pretend not to notice. She'd never atoned for her absence; the pain of it weighed down every word between them. But still she wanted to hear the line crackle with loaded silence; resentment, smugness, an unwavering refusal to see each other's points of view – it all felt a lot like love.

A ping came then: confirmation from her airline that all flights – including hers, booked for the day after tomorrow – would be grounded until the storm passed. She turned from the anger rippling through the foyer, readied her keycard between shaking fingers.

Her mother picked up on the sixth ring. 'Well, this is unexpected.'

'Hey, Mum.'

'Hang on, I'm just getting off the bus,' her mother said. Away from the phone, Lily heard the heavy hiss of the bus doors opening.

'Oh, sorry,' Lily said. There was a two-hour time difference; it was just after lunch there. 'I didn't realise you were out.'

'Don't worry. But anyway, what's going on? My birthday's not for another three months.'

Lily lowered herself to the carpeted floor of her room, leaned a bare leg against the window. 'I know, I just . . . I don't always need a reason, do I?'

Her mother sounded cautious. 'No, I suppose not.'

Lily heard the tolling of a bell. 'Where are you?'

'I'm on that green, you know, by the posh nursery? Just looking for a free bench.'

She pictured the park, but when she tried to imagine the feeling of the grass underfoot, her mind brought up wet sand instead. 'Do you remember the scarlet ibises? At the bird sanctuary, when we went to—?'

Her mother cut her off. 'You called just to ask me that?'

On the other side of the window, the snow had started up again, falling in quiet flakes. She told the truth. 'It just came to me.'

'Yes, I remember,' her mother said. She sounded tired now, and very far away. 'Beautiful birds.'

In the boundless white, Lily thought she saw flashes of red.

\*

The attendees filtered into the auditorium and took their seats. Lily had slept badly; the air in her room had swirled, humid and thick, at odds with the snow outside. There's a storm brewing, her mother would say. She hadn't mentioned the snow in the end, or the tropical climate that clung to her body like an embrace. Even now, as she smoothed a hand over the stiff fabric of her skirt, she could feel it, wrapped around her waist and ankles, tethering her to an in-between place where memory became sensory. The storm brewed inside her. She no longer felt ashamed of its presence; it was a part of her, far more real than the world that was steadily disintegrating in front of her – the world of boardrooms and spreadsheets she'd tried so hard to make home.

She'd been caught in a downpour once in Madrid. Rain had pummelled cafe awnings and left the cobbled paths gleaming. She'd taken shelter in the alcoved entrance of a restaurant and watched waiters ferry salt cellars and napkin dispensers from the outdoor tables inside. Eventually, they seemed to stop caring about the deluge, moving as though the sky were completely clear. Later, she remembered it as though it had been a dream: so much rain, but all she'd felt was dry heat pressing at the back of her neck.

One of the organisers appeared onstage, prompting a wave of chatter to rise and fall across the audience. 'Thank you all for giving us some of your time before the morning conference,' he said. 'We know these last few days have been fraught with uncertainty, so we wanted to briefly address what will be happening as a result of the ongoing unfavourable weather.'

Lily tried to focus on the words that came next: cancelled flights, airlines, complimentary rooms and meals. They seemed, however, to be meant for someone else, a version of herself she had shed, left exoskeletal in a grave of snow. To her new ears, they were muffled, jostling with the sound of blood-red wings slicing through wetland air. 'This is such a drag,' the person beside her said, words projected with the hope of being heard, a net cast wide. She could scarcely lift her chin to nod.

Two rows down, she could see a woman using her name badge to fan cool air onto her neck. A man at the end of the row had undone the top button of his shirt, a dark patch of sweat blooming between his shoulder blades. Their discomfort was infectious: soon, the entire auditorium swarmed with the movement of loosened ties and hair pushed off faces. The organiser frowned. 'Evidently, something is wrong with the heating. We'll get to that right away, but perhaps for now if you could all make your way—'

The attendees stood and moved towards the exits in a state of controlled panic. The room felt smaller, tighter; a shrinking bird's cage, latch finally unhooked. On the floor beneath Lily were dozens of lanyards, moulted feathers marked with names no one knew. She thought about the downpour in Madrid. Had the waiters sensed it too, the climatic changeling, heat where there should have been rain?

They spilled into the foyer, wanting for cool air to down like a glass of cold water, but the same liquid heat warped the teak-panelled walls of the room. Outside, the shape of things was returning. The recognisable lines of a working society – the edges of pavement, streetlights spaced evenly apart – were visible again, because the sky had cleared. Because, Lily saw as she moved with the crowd towards the wall of glass, it was no longer snowing, but raining: a deluge of water falling from heavy clouds. In the moist air, she saw scarlet wings bright against the sky, a formation of ibises bound for somewhere else.

'Have you ever seen anything like it?' the blond man said, suddenly beside her, shirt undone to his stomach.

'I have,' Lily said, and again she saw the lush hilltops peeking out above the clouds. She pressed her palms against the glass and felt droplets of mist settle on the backs of her hands.

# Sand Castles

We're standing in the kitchen when the first tremors hit. Virginia is already crying but when the ground starts to move she grabs my hand and pulls me down under the table. Above us, things fall. A glass full of water shatters on the floor and my sheet music slips from its folder.

'Granny?' I shout over the sound of the shuddering walls.

Her voice comes, fragmented, from the bedroom. 'Maddy, stay right where you are, I'll be fine.'

In the sink, dishes fracture. I should have washed them last night. The draining rack shakes all the cutlery loose and a sea of forks clatters towards us. I grip the sticky lino with my fingers and watch the pattern of artificial light change as the lamp swings from the ceiling.

I can just about hear Granny through the open door. 'What did I say, Maddy? Didn't I tell you one was coming?'

'Yes, Granny, you did. You were right.'

'I could feel it in my bones, Maddy. I always feel it like that.'

Virginia puts her hand over mine but I can't look at her, not yet.

It had been a warm winter, so everyone kept saying; weather that had made us all act out in one way or another. Edie Allan had shaved her head for a dare and been suspended, and at least three girls from Year 10 were rumoured to have got into some rooftop bar in Te Aro with fake IDs. If I'd done anything out of line it was strictly accidental. Virginia thought it was funny how I freaked out every time I risked a disciplinary by association to her or one of the others. 'It's final year, Scholarship Susie,' she'd said to me earlier that week while she lit up a joint at the back of the sports field. 'Stop being so uptight, eh.'

That day, I woke up before Virginia, and I lay there in her bed staring up at the ceiling, which she'd begged her mum to let her have wallpapered with this really pretty cloud-print paper that was probably really expensive. I could hear Lois doing mum things in the kitchen: opening and closing the fridge and the cupboards, shaking the cereal box to check enough was left for us both. This was our first sleepover since they'd moved to the penthouse, and Lois had given me a tour like it was one of the properties on her company portfolio. Marble en-suites with waterfall showers, entertainment room with state-of-the-art cinema system. On the terrace, the harbour lights had twinkled; the water felt close enough to touch.

Virginia lay on her side facing away from me. We'd been having sleepovers since we were ten; always at her place, but never if she had her period, because on those nights she wanted to sleep alone. Virginia's hair was that colour you can only get by dropping a few hundred dollars at the salon: melted butter mixed with cinnamon and brown sugar, and it smelled like that too. She'd dyed my hair once; a cool flush of violet one night when Lois was working late at an open house in Island Bay. Her fingers foaming the product into my scalp felt better than anything I'd felt before, like how I imagine I might have felt in my mother's womb: held, safe, loved.

In her bathroom, I pulled off my t-shirt and fastened my bra at the front of my stomach before swivelling it round and tugging my arms through the holes. I was very good at replacing bad thoughts about my body with bad thoughts about cello, so when it occurred to me that the hairs on my belly looked weird, I started thinking about the audition instead. I hadn't practiced the Bach enough – Granny had been ill and the sound of it had bothered her – and I was no good at sight reading and they were probably going to tell me then and there that I sucked.

'Are you nervous?'

Virginia's reflection appeared next to mine in the mirror. 'I just want to get it over with.'

'You've always known what you wanted, Maddy,' Lois said at breakfast, when Virginia explained why I wouldn't be in school that morning. She kept nodding and frowning, like maybe she was jealous or surprised. 'It must be wonderful to have that level of focus. Maybe some of it might rub off on Vee here.'

Virginia poured more milk into her cereal bowl, sloshing some over the side. She wiped at the spillage with the wrist of her blazer. 'Give it a rest, would you, Lois.'

I drank my orange juice, licking the pulp off my lip. Later, Virginia swiped absent fingers over her phone screen as we leaned over the wall on the terrace. 'I just think it'll be good for me, you know,' she said.

'You don't think you'll get bored?'

She looked towards the harbour, like it was her own private marina, every yacht and sailboat a royal subject. 'Of dragging myself out of bed to analyse books I haven't read and facts I won't remember? I'll be fine.'

On the beach below us, a woman wearing matching sportswear was walking a tiny Chihuahua. 'It must be nice,' I said. My voice sounded pointed. Spiteful.

Virginia smiled at me. The breeze picked up a lock of hair and tacked it to her lip gloss. 'What's that?'

I'd been with her when she'd pocketed that gloss at the mall, a nineties brown that smelled like milk chocolate. 'To get to be perfectly mediocre.'

It was a thing we did, throwing sharp comments at each other and hoping that the shards of truth were buried deep enough not to leave marks. 'You know, this place could be worth so much money,' Virginia had said to me when we'd hung out at mine after school one afternoon last week. 'If it wasn't such a dump.' We'd been sitting on the porch, looking out at the hills that flanked the valley. 'Beautiful view, though,' she'd added, and when she'd nestled her head into the crook of my neck the sting of her words had faded.

The waves sloshed against the shore as the moment stretched out, until finally Virginia turned around. 'Haven't you got an audition to fail?' she said as she walked away.

Our house was on the dark side of the valley. The lack of sunlight condensed on the walls, forming in cold droplets that turned into bursts of black mould that I wiped away routinely. Granny was sure that the damp had ruined her lungs. Some days, she could barely get a word out before the coughing and retching started up. Her room was a mess of fans and dehumidifying units, generating a constant whirr that I'd come to associate exclusively with home. 'This house is killing me,' Granny would say, but she'd never leave. It was where we'd both been born, and where my mother had died, and sometimes it felt like her mission to purify the air was as much to do with her health as it was a way of letting go of the pain that dwelled here.

She was sitting at the top of the porch steps when I got home, the weak sun glowing in her bleached blonde crop. She often did this in the mornings, and in the time it took to drink her black coffee she'd fill up on new complaints. 'The weatherboard's peeling, see, look there,' she said to me as I walked up the hill. 'And these bushes, well, we'd be better off pulling them up and starting again I reckon.'

I squeezed past her on the steps, bent to kiss the crown of her head. 'Good morning, Granny.'

Mum had died in the kitchen. I was three years old when it happened, which was convenient for Granny, because it enabled her to change the details with every retelling and I'd never really known what was truth or myth. 'Your mother was an addict,' she told me on my thirteenth birthday. 'That's the crux of it, Maddy.' Each year invited a new fabrication, and by the time I turned seventeen I had an encyclopaedic knowledge of all the ways a mother could die; a Rolodex of reasons to choose from depending on what I wanted to believe on any given day.

In the sink, days' worth of dishes were piled up, crusted remnants of pasta sauce stuck to the sides. I should have cleaned them last night, I thought, before I went to Virginia's. I plucked the Bach from the pile of sheet music on the table and stuffed it in the pocket of Cindy's – my cello's – case.

Granny had never liked Virginia. 'Little Miss Princess,' she always called her. 'I should have never let you go to that fancy school. You'd do better among your own kind.' I wanted so badly for none of it to matter.

'There's an earthquake coming, Maddy,' Granny said now, shuffling into the kitchen.

'How do you know that, Granny?'

'Oh, you know, I can feel it. Something in the air, a heaviness in the bones.' She lowered herself into one of the folding chairs at the table with a groan that seemed to come from deep within her. 'You always look so smart in that uniform of yours.'

My hand went to the pleat of the scratchy woollen skirt, to the patch of hair I'd missed just above my knee.

'It's going to be a big one, Maddy. Be careful out there.'

'Are we just not going to talk about what happened?' Virginia raises her voice over the rumbling sound of objects falling away from shelves. I try to move my hand from under hers but she curls her fingers between mine.

A metallic crash comes from the bedroom. I picture the network of fans and wires, a floor of snakes trembling with every wave of movement.

'Can it wait until after?' I say, red-hot tears clouding my voice.

'I don't know, I don't know,' Virginia sobs.

I think about Cindy. I'd left her leaning against the side of my bed. If the shelves shuck their books loose, they'll land on the bridge, snap her strings off for sure. My knees feel like they're lifting off the ground with every shudder. I make myself heavy, belly close to the floor like a cat primed to pounce on its prey.

This isn't our first earthquake but it's the strongest that we can remember.

\*

Under the domed ceiling of the planetarium, I imagined I was floating in outer space. The curved screens projected a vast, endless sky, shot through with trillions of stars. Cindy, wedged between the rows of seats, seemed so strange and meaningless against a universe with no beginning or end. Maybe I'd known this all along; maybe it had come out in every note I'd played at the audition, every finger I'd lifted from the bridge and tried to put back into a place that I thought made sense but was actually completely inconsequential. I leaned back in my plush chair and lost myself in the make-believe void.

Virginia's footsteps were soft but quick. She sat down next to me, dumped her school bag on the floor and took a long, deep breath in. 'Well?'

'There's no way I'm getting in after that.'

'Yeah right, you're getting in, just you wait.'

A glint of light filtered in as two young boys opened the door to leave. I listened to the slow brush of the heavy door as it eventually closed. 'Don't you ever think, it's all so fucking pointless? Like, we're all just going around in our stupid bodies doing stupid shit in the middle of this massive fucking universe that could flip the switch on us any second?'

Virginia angled herself towards me. I could smell her hair and feel the warmth and weight of her presence beside me as if it had its own gravitational pull. 'Look at me,' she said, her knee knocking mine. When I didn't turn around, she reached out a hand and drew my chin to face her. 'Sure, the universe could flip its switch and kill us all instantly. You could get hit by a car tomorrow or fall and break your neck. An earthquake could come along and flatten the whole island.'

'This isn't really cheering me up, Vee.'

'Sorry, sorry,' she said, retracting her hand. 'The point is, that's what makes life worth living. We never know when it might end. So we go out every day and try to do our best and make things happen for ourselves because what the hell else is there to do but—'

In the split second that followed, our mouths collided, then, just as quickly, pulled apart. In the blacks of Virginia's eyes, I saw exploding stars reflected. 'Did you just . . .' she said, touching her fingers to her bottom lip.

My stomach churned as the simulated sky shifted above us, distant planets coming into view. 'I'm sorry. I don't know why I—'

But then it was happening again, and I gripped the velvet chair arm between us and closed my eyes to find a boundless starlit sky there, too.

Millions of years before I existed, fault lines shifted in seismic waves, pushing the ground our house stands on into the shape of the valley it takes today. We'll talk about it later, how the lives we carve out of the moving ground are nothing but sand castles. On the news, they'll report on magnitudes, damage, risks and repairs. But under the table, our bare knees bruising against the floor, we are silent when the tremors stop.

'Don't move,' Granny shouts. 'Aftershocks.'

Tears drop from my face onto the lino. I think about Mum, and the statistical inevitability that she once used this table for shelter from an earthquake too, maybe even when she was my age. I think about how alive she might have felt, and that she might have been scared of dying, like we all are, but that death was coming for her anyway, like it's coming for us all. My arms and back start to shake, as if my body is made up of faults, every sob its own wave of motion. 'I want to do it again,' I say.

Outside, car alarms blare like a chorus of flightless mechanical birds. I arch my back and feel it touch against the underside of the table, the metal legs jolting in response. I can feel the tears subsiding, a numbness washing into their place. Next to me, Virginia pulls her phone from her blazer's inside pocket and scans a thumb over the screen which has somehow stayed intact. 'Is your mum safe?' I ask her.

She lets out a sigh. 'She's fine.'

'I can hear you girls moving,' Granny yells. The sound of her voice, also intact, is almost enough to set me off again.

'I'm sorry I called you mediocre,' I say.

Virginia's hand is growing heavy over mine. She gives it a slow squeeze. 'I'm sorry I called your house a dump. That was so messed up of me.'

I raise my head and look out at the kitchen floor, littered with broken things. 'It kind of is one now,' I say.

Virginia laughs. 'Yeah, I guess it is.'

On the car alarms go. I try to imagine how the air will sound once they stop, but I can't. It feels like everything has changed, like we've slipped through to a parallel world; the world that has been waiting for us, waiting to break through the cracks in our walls and floors and in the crust of the earth itself.

'I want to, too,' Virginia says. 'Do it again, I mean.'

Finally, I look at her. 'OK,' I say.

'OK,' she says back, voice so small I hardly hear it over the car alarms that ring on and on, an orchestra of noise in this, our new universe.

# We Will Know
# What To Do

You find me waist-deep in the water, clothes in a pile on the sanded bank.

'Cate, what are you doing? It's the middle of the night.'

I'm not sure how you heard me. I'd tried so hard to be quiet, creeping bare-footed across the boards of the jetty to the lake. I turn towards the shore and the glow of light behind my cabin door. 'I just wanted to go in, just quickly.' My voice sounds jagged, too loud.

Behind you, the tree line looms against the still-light midnight sky. 'It couldn't wait until the morning?'

I stipple the side of my thigh, slow-fingered under the water. 'I guess it could've.'

Neither of us move. I think about the way your body felt next to mine in this same lake yesterday.

'Well,' you say, receding. 'I'll leave you alone. But be careful – there are leeches.'

'I'll be careful,' I say, slipping my feet down into the silt.

I haven't always been a careful person. I was reckless once, a lit match thrown into the wind. An urge to destroy doesn't put itself out; its flames are not eventually stifled. I carry its embers with me, glowing phosphorescent. I haven't been careful with you.

I wait for the gentle click of your cabin door closing before I wade back onto the sand and collect my clothes. Inside my cabin, I sit on the edge of the camping bed and breathe raggedly into deep silence. The thin frame aches under my weight, metal whining in protest. I touch my thigh again, with a desperate hope that is shattered as soon as I feel it, still there: crusted fronds that have burst from my skin like a cluster of unshaved hairs.

We arrive at the clear-cut early the next day, a cool lilt in the morning heat that we know won't last for long. You hang back while I erect a perimeter around the area of study, batting mosquitos away from your face. For someone from this place, you seem ill-equipped for its pests. I adjust the netting on my hat, feel your eyes on me in the sun that touches everything, no canopy left to dapple it. I measure the study plot's ground moisture level, note down its coordinates on my clipboard. Already, I notice the lichen I've come to observe, spread across the stumps, kaleidoscopic. I want to learn how they adapt in the face of habitat destruction, or, as you put it, 'management'. In the coming months, herds of reindeer will roam the indigenous forests north of here, looking for nourishing wisps of arboreal lichen draped on the branches of spruce and pine, still standing at the mercy of the logging company you work for. I bend to look more closely at the stumps. The patches of wood between the bodies of lichen are smooth and pale, not yet marked by the passing of time.

'When were these trees cut?' I ask.

You scratch at a bite that swells on the side of your neck. 'About six months ago, maybe?'

A tightness spreads across my chest. 'Six months?'

'That's quite quick, isn't it, for them to be so advanced,' you say.

Above us, the wings of a circling hawk are black against the sunburned sky. 'Yes. Very quick.'

'That's good, right?' you say. Unguarded hopefulness quivers in your voice. 'They're adapting to our logging activities.'

'This species normally favours soil over wood as its substrate,' I say.

'So, it's evolving?'

I peer through the hand lens that hangs on a leather string around my neck. Under its amplified sight, the brittle grey branches are clustered, nebulous. 'Will you pass me the collection kit?'

You don't move at first, and it occurs to me that you must feel like your presence here is only as chaperone. You're fulfilling a role you've been assigned, one that doesn't allow for the sharing or owning of knowledge, any wisdom you might have to impart replaced by inflexible company lines. Eventually, you hand me the backpack with the knife and paper pouches inside, leaning over my shoulder as I carve a segment of the lichen away and slip it into a pouch.

Crouched by the tree stump, I don't notice you reaching your arm under the perimeter until you are stroking the small of my back. 'Hey,' you say, with a familiarity that empties the breath from my lungs. I stand up too quickly, my clipboard clattering to the ground.

'Did I do something wrong?' you say.

Everything about this is wrong, but under the pressing hand of the forest's unshaded heat, I want to kiss you, and I do.

We continue the field work in silence, performing a cautious choreography that keeps us apart from each other. I chisel fragments of wood away from colonised stumps and you hold open the paper pouch into which I drop the collected specimens. Fear and excitement twist into knots in my stomach. I want to tell you my early conclusions, but they're tangled in the wasteland between science and something murkier, less bound by the rules of what we already know. You look at your watch with no pretence of subtlety. The distance between us measures wider than the physical boundaries we've etched in the soil.

By the time we are done at this plot, it is thirty-three degrees, and the midday sun sits high and unforgiving in its cloudless sky. We roll down every window in the car, blast cool air onto our knees. The road is quiet and arid, gravel flying up from under the wheels and pinging off the bonnet. 'I want to show you something,' you say, turning us onto a narrow dirt path. You park by the side of a lake, its placid surface green with the reflections of the pine trees that line the bank. You take the few metres to the water in loping strides, as though you know the distance intimately; pull off your t-shirt and jeans, leave your socks in a bundle by your shoes. I try not to stare at the freckles strewn across your back, the rings of red skin where your t-shirt sleeves end. Ripples spread like waves around you and you shout out in wonder. 'Join me,' you say.

Under my trousers, the shrubby growth bristles. 'I'm OK,' I say, sitting down on the sparse grass bank.

Your country is one of water: liquid bodies scattered across it. Days earlier, in the lake by our cabins, I kissed you for the first time. The strangeness of our touching melted away in the seconds it took for you to pull me into the curve of you.

'I'm a good person, you know,' you say now, bobbing on the fly-pocked surface. As you float through the languorous water, you almost look like someone I could trust.

What you don't know about me is that, as a girl, I threw several lit matches into a neighbour's hedge in the deep of a summer night and ran into the woods to watch the flames from a distance. My skin burns with the desire to tell you this as we lie on the floor of your cabin. In the heat of the late afternoon, I let myself remember the release I used to find in fire. I wonder what you would think of me if I gave you this side of myself. I've given so much of myself already, and you seem grateful, conscious of what you could lose. This, I'm sure, would tip the scale, loosen my footing on the tightrope, open water waiting for my fall.

'I got lost in these woods, once,' you say, staring up at the cobwebbed ceiling.

Details unfold: you'd been on a fishing trip with your older brother, wandered off like little boys do. Perhaps, you admit, there'd been a part of you that had wanted to be lost, prove to yourself and everyone else that you were strong enough to go it alone. You'd picked handfuls of blueberries off their bushes, looked for edible resin oozing from the trunks of pine trees. When I ask you how long you were gone for, you frown. 'Just a few hours,' you say, and from the hollow sound of your voice I can tell that I shouldn't ask any more questions.

'When did you become so interested in the natural world?' you ask me.

Through the old, blurred glass of the window, the sun glints like a flame. 'When I saw just how capable we are of destroying it.'

You come from a long line of woodsmen: wordless, strong-armed men, hands whittled rough by the work. You feel that your work is important: managing the conservation efforts of the big, bad logging company your forefathers come from; a friendly face to charm tourists and journalists, scientists and botanists like me. You talk about the many livelihoods dependent on the steady work of logging, thinking about your own family, its lineage rooted in cutting and stripping. You're so earnest in your beliefs, like a child clinging on to a fairy tale they suspect to be only half true. 'Maybe that's what you think I'm doing,' you say, as we braid our fingers together and hold them up towards the cabin door. 'Destroying nature.'

My body stiffens, irritation blooming red across my cheeks. 'I don't think that,' I say, untangling my hand from yours.

'Actually, I'm trying to change things, just like you are.'

'And how are you trying to do that?' I ask.

You look at me then, blue eyes like pools. 'Sometimes, change isn't a radical thing. Sometimes it has to be quiet and slow, and speak the right language.'

The space between us sags, something like pity taking shape within it. 'You must have been scared, in the woods,' I say.

You close your eyes. 'It was just a few hours.'

In the silence that follows, a heaviness weighs down on me. Field work makes for drowsy afternoons, but this tiredness seems to pull from another source. The temptation to succumb feels overwhelming; an elemental force I'm not sure I want to resist. In cautious acquiescence, I let my eyelids flutter closed. On my leg, I know the growth is spreading, branching dryly across a warm, soft plane.

You lean your body over mine to kiss me. 'I don't feel well, I'm sorry,' I say, easing myself from under you.

You drape an arm across your forehead. 'You know, Cate, you should tell me if you don't want to do this. We can stop.'

The ghost of your lips sits wet on my mouth. 'I can't tell you that.'

'Why not?'

'Because it wouldn't be true.'

I walk across the thin lawn that separates our cabins, wondering what it might become if it were left to grow wild. Once I'm inside, I strip down to my underwear and twist to see that the lichen has multiplied across the underside of my thigh; if I bend to my haunches, the lengths of its branches scratch at the backs of my knees. Panic starts to close around my throat. I reach for my clipboard on the small wooden table by the window, catching its corner with the palm of my hand and knocking it onto the floor. I pull the pen cap loose with my teeth and scrape my shins against the floorboards as I curl over to scribble my findings on the clipboard where it has landed. This is the only thing I can think to do.

I drift in and out of a restless sleep, coiled on the floor of the cabin. At twilight, I wake to the groaning of the jetty under human feet, a smooth splash as the surface of the lake breaks to your shape. I pull on my trousers, not looking at the lichen, and walk out to the shore. In the water, you are scrubbing at your shoulder, your body coiled. You jolt when you see me, hold up your hands. 'Don't come any closer, Cate. It could be infectious.'

I remember then, the burning air through the oaks; the thrill that had quelled the guilt. The ground we grew from has been levelled, its moral boundaries blurred. Again, I step out of my trousers, and as I stride ever nearer to the end of the sandbank your shouts of protest dwindle. You meet me in the shallows, press a hand to your mouth. Your eyes run the length of my thigh. 'What is happening to us?'

Gently, I push at your arm until your body yields, turning. On you, it has spread in a powdered formation, like worn velvet. When I lift my fingers to touch it, you flinch. 'It's the lichen. It's using us,' I say.

'We need to see a doctor,' you say, displacing the water as you wade away. 'This could be dangerous.'

'It's using our bodies as substrates,' I say. 'It's almost as if it's trying to tell us something.'

The lake drips off you in glistening rivulets. 'Can you hear yourself?'

I think about the sickness that claimed me after the fire had gone out; the weeks I spent bed-bound, wrestling with a darkness inside me that was determined to take root. The thicket of thoughts that had formed at the clear-cut starts to untangle. 'When we cause harm, there are consequences. There's a response, and we have to listen to it. We have to listen to what it tries to teach us.'

You scoff; a choked, fearful sound. I pull on my trousers and scramble towards the cabin. Inside, I grab at essentials – shoes, shirt, water canteen – and head back outside. You follow me as I walk towards the tree line. 'Where are you going?'

I reach the woods and turn to face you. 'You wanted to know how I made this my work, my life. I listened. Nature had something to teach me, and instead of being afraid, instead of running away and hiding behind what I thought I knew, I ran towards it.'

We look at each other, then: deeply, as though staring into a clear pool of water or the ever-glowing embers of a fire.

\*

Around me, the forest thickens. The ground shifts, springy moss to cobbled soil; soon, there is no discernible path, only the ways that deer and moose have wandered. I follow their routes, branches and bracken stroking at me in the gathering dark. The lichen grows in circular patterns, dusted on the trunks of pine and birch and the sides of huge rocks that tower towards the sky. As I move deeper into the woods, it too seems to move, a creeping motion in the corner of my eye.

I hear you in snapped twigs and brushed away leaves, and the eventual calling out of my name. You're begging me to slow down, but I don't, not until I reach it: a clearing, like a graveyard, the left-behind stumps like headstones to mark the trees which once stood there. In the distance, a solitary pine tree is ribboned in logging tape, its curled branches drooping. I keep going until I'm at its base, trunk wide and thick with hundreds of years' worth of growth. I sit at its feet between two dense roots that gnarl from the ground. The air is cool and clouded with gnats, the darkening sky illuminating its own version of reality.

'What are you trying to prove, Cate?' you say, knees and back bent as you catch your breath. 'How is this going to help?'

I feel raw as wounded flesh, the way I felt that night you found me in the water. 'Honestly, I don't know,' I say, pushing my back against the tree. 'It just feels like the right place to be.'

Your limbs buzz with agitation, both hands through your hair and legs turning, then turning back. 'I can't leave you here.'

'Then don't.'

For a moment, you don't move, and I think you might stay. My stomach churns with this possibility, because your being here feels vital to my own, a symbiotic healing connecting us, transcending difference or desire. Maybe you understand this too, because you don't leave; you pick your way through the shrubs, heavy with young blueberries, until you are on the other side of the tree, where you lower yourself to the ground and push your back against the same ancient bark.

We each take a deep breath in, then out. 'So what do we do now?' you ask.

'We listen.'

The sounds of the clear-cut are many: clawed creatures scuttling across the forest floor, the faraway calls of owls, unseen wings spanning outwards. From the thicket come the cries of foxes, or deer; terrifying grumblings of another world. Invertebrates tread with a blood-stopping touch across my hands and the back of my neck, but I stay still, take it all in. Time means something else here. It's slow and quick, non-existent and ever-present, containing and expanding itself in the spaces between every thing.

When the sky is as dark as it'll get, I hear you start to cry. Your tears come out in a whimper; a strained sound, jarring in its rawness. I wonder at the memories that are reeled against the insides of your eyelids right now, the truths that are stirring up sadness, or grief. I wonder if you still feel lost among trees, if you haven't yet found your way home.

I grasp at my thoughts but they scatter away from me like ants fleeing disturbed ground. My thigh throbs. I fold my legs up against my chest, press my palms to the solid earth. Then, something starts to take shape at the edge of my senses. A girl. She's pressed in the gaps between my hands and the ground; in the grooves of the bark and the delicate undersides of moonlit leaves. She hasn't always relied on a destructive release, wasn't born wanting to watch things burn. The need was forged in the world around her, in the absence and violence of others. Here, the marshland becomes too treacherous to cross; remembered terrain that will close itself around me if I dare descend any further into its depths. So I turn back and into myself, towards the girl who lit the match, who delighted in the wooden smell of the flame.

Around us, the forest breathes. I think I hear your shoes shifting in the dirt, knees crunching to stand, but you never appear. On the other side of the ancient tree, you sit like a counterweight on the end of a scale; like this, we tether each other in place. Like this, we are mirrors, reflecting each other's guilt, shame, fear, the rest of it all. We reflect the forest, too: its pines and birches and spruces cut short or bowed by force, the persistent renewal of berries and fungi against the odds we set. I think like this, widely and sensually, while the sky rearranges above us; until, eventually, birdsong lifts the sun over the stumps to brush its light across their crusted tops. I push my hand under my waistband and feel for the lichen. Behind me, you're doing the same thing, gripping at the neck of your shirt and pawing the skin there. The sound of your laugh melts into the morning chorus, and I let mine join in, too.

We walk to the edge of the clear-cut and find an overgrown forest path, faint tyre tracks like ghosts of past explorers. We don't know where this path will take us but we walk it; curious, open. Dew dots our ankles and pale-winged butterflies flutter close to the ground. Ahead of us, two rusted roofs glint in the sun, and we quicken our pace, loosening with the relief of being somewhere familiar. I am not the same person I was when I left here last night; not the same person who stood in this lake and wished away inescapable truths. In the middle of the lawn between the cabins, you pull me into an embrace. Your shoulders slacken and I feel the pulse in your neck against the side of my face. I wonder if you, too, can sense it; that we've become different versions of ourselves, born again in the dark.

'I want it to be over,' you say, and there are so many things you could mean.

We don't talk about what we heard in the night, or how our bodies felt as the lichen receded. We won't, as we navigate the last days of field work; even as we say our inevitable goodbye, exchanging chaste pecks on the cheek. Then, when we're returned to our disparate worlds, when we are sitting at desks or cutting between glass and concrete buildings as tall as trees, or hiding our darkness from others, we will feel it, the lichen, inching across our scalps or on the flats of our feet. We will be calm when this happens, because this time, we will know. This time, we will know what to do.

# *Acknowledgements*

I began writing the stories that make up this collection in 2018, but am grateful to many people and organisations whose support both preceded and extended beyond this time.

Firstly, Abby and Bridie at Dear Damsels, for creating a supportive, inclusive space that has championed my writing for many years. Their encouragement and insight have helped shape these stories and many before them. Thank you to the moon and back. Additional thanks to Elise Bateman for creating a cover illustration that so perfectly captures the nature of this collection, and everyone involved in the editing, proofing and typesetting processes that have brought this book into its beautiful physical form.

Many thanks to Mish Green and the February 2021 cohort of the Comma Press Short Story Course, whose guidance moved *The Creek House* across the Atlantic Ocean, and to the judges of the Cambridge Short Story Prize 2021 for including it on their longlist.

I owe a massive debt of gratitude to Kerry Ryan, whose Write Like A Grrrl courses not only introduced me to a community of writers I hadn't known I needed, but connected me to lifelong friends, too. Kerry's personal input and endless compassion have made me the writer I am today. Additional thanks to For Books' Sake for doing such vital work, and to Elspeth Wilson and the May 2021 class of Write Nature Like A Grrrl for providing fertile soil for these stories to sprout in.

To my Write Like A Grrrl soul sisters: what would become of me without you? For every overpriced Southbank Centre coffee, every life chat that spilled into workshopping time, every WhatsApp message of encouragement and congratulations: thank you. And special thanks in particular to Jess Glaisher and Isha Karki whose feedback and support mean the world.

Thank you, also, to my family and friends. To Ma, for reading us David Almond in bed for longer than is perhaps considered normal. To Pa, for never once doubting I'd get here. To my sisters, Hannah and Tracey, and my besties, especially my fellow writing buddy Tara Costello, for their cheerleading and advice throughout this process.

Stefan, what magic is at play that makes the simple statement 'You can do it!' quite so powerful when you say it? Thank you for always understanding, perhaps more deeply than I have myself at times, what I'm capable of when I set my mind to it. I'm endlessly grateful for the space and support you've given me to work towards this dream.

To the characters on these pages: thank you for trusting me to share your stories. I have savoured the time I've spent listening to and unravelling your pasts, desires, flaws and fears. You may be fictional, but you've felt very real to me.

Lastly, to Planet Earth; to the magpies that hop around the garden, the blackcurrants that ripen on the ancient bush, the meteoric lakes that accommodate my body every summer. Some of the places in these stories are ones I know and love; others are places I hope to one day visit. Planet Earth, thank you for being a creative muse, a storyteller, a life sustainer. I, we, owe you so much.

## *What She's Having:*
## *Stories of Women and Food*

Food is about so much more than just the first bite . . .

What we eat can fill us up, satisfy our needs or leave us hungry for more.
It connects us to our culture, defines our routines and flavours our fondest memories.

Whole stories are made across a dinner table, and in *What She's Having*,
sixteen writers explore the complex and meaningful relationships that women
have with the food we cook, eat and share.

Bringing together fiction, non-fiction and poetry, this collection
of women's stories about food is something to savour.

## Let Me Know When You're Home:
## Stories of Female Friendship

What is it that makes female friendship so special / complex / intense / important / messy / supportive / essential?

From growing up together to growing apart, from the oldest of friends to the fake ones, our relationships with other women can be our greatest loves. They can also be difficult, elusive and the source of our deepest heartbreaks.

In *Let Me Know When You're Home*, fifteen women writers look at female friendship in all its forms, in a collection of fiction, non-fiction and poetry that is both a frank exploration of these relationships and a true celebration of what women can achieve with the support of each other.

# dear damsels

**your words | your stories | your collective**

**deardamsels.com**

- deardamsels
- deardamsels
- deardamsels